PROLOGUE

YEAR 1

LORDS
READING
ORDER

YEAR 2

YEAR 3

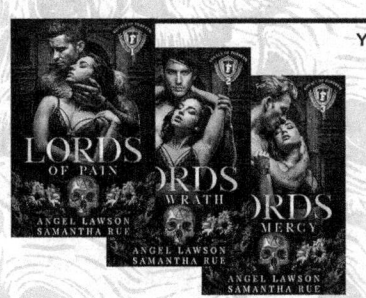

LORDS

YEAR 4

DUKES

EPILOGUE

PRINCES

YEAR 5

LEGEND

 LORDS BROWNSTONE

 FORSYTH UNIVERSITY CAMPUS

 DUKES CLOCK TOWER

 PRINCES PURPLE PALACE

1. DANIEL'S HOUSE

2. THE AVENUE

3. THE VELVET HIDEAWAY

4. MERCER FIELD

5. MERCER MANOR

6. CRANE MOTEL

7. SHOOTING FIELD

8. DUKES GYM

9. DANIEL'S OFFICE BUILDING

SHE WAS

supposed

to be

mine

THE BACK
STORY

ΔΔΖ

ANGEL LAWSON
SAMANTHA RUE

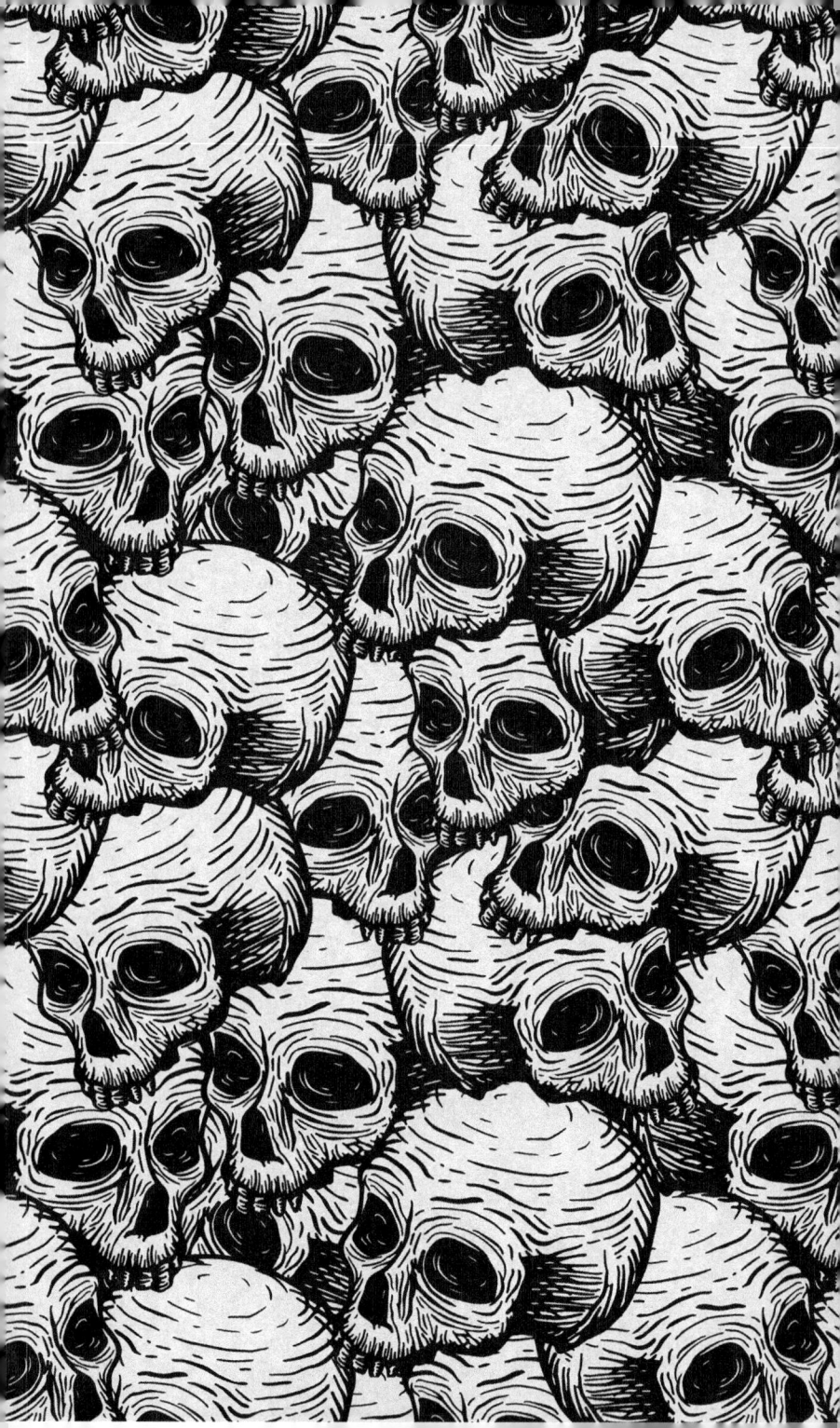

TRISTIAN
MERCER

1

TRAPPING

"Look dude, you know what they say." Rath is reclined back on the couch, a controller in his hand as a bottle of beer balances between his knees. "The best way to get over a girl is to get under another one."

"Stick to instrumentals, Rath. Your poetic sentiments need some refining." I push my nail under the corner of the sticker on the bottle of beer I'm holding, trying to downplay the inferno happening in my chest. I can't hold it against them for not understanding. The closest thing to a relationship these two have ever had was probably with their own hands. Instead, I go for something they're more likely to appreciate. "Here's what I want to know. How does someone who's as big a whore as Gen have the fucking *gall* to refuse me head?"

There's a chorus of groans. "Jesus. You still on about that?" Rath shakes his head, and then scowls—not at me, but at the game he's playing on the screen. "She let you fuck her pussy and ass. Why are you so hung up about head?"

The inferno rages and churns, and I don't say what should be obvious. It's the principle. That bitch belongs on her knees before me. She should have worshipped me. In no universe should a Mercer want for something. It's just not fucking natural.

"Because he likes them on their knees." Killian says, only half paying attention. "It's a power play. The sick fuck wants to watch them choke on his dick."

Okay, maybe it *is* obvious.

"And now she's shacked up on that asshole's boat. A *boat*. A house that floats on water?" I flick the lighter and wave the flame under the wrapper, setting the paper on fire. I watch as it sizzles and catches life, burning fast, but holding onto it until the flame licks my fingertips. But it doesn't compare to the fire within. The licking flames. The explosive pyrotechnics. "I'm a goddamn Mercer. I could have given her anything she wanted."

"Are you, like…hurt about this?" Rath asks, trying to figure it out. "Don't tell me you were in love with that skank."

"God no. *No*." Gen isn't the kind of girl you love. She's the kind of girl you make plans with because it's convenient. But that isn't the fucking point. There's a light series of thumps above our head, drawing my attention. "Your parent's home?" Jesus, the last thing I need is to deal with Killer's dad right now. I don't think I'd have it in me to be nice.

"You hoping Killer's stepmom will suck your cock?" Rath's mouth tugs into a dark smirk. "I bet she's good at it."

He's not wrong. Daniel brought home his new wife a little over a year ago and it's no secret she was a prostitute. A hot one. Her tits are fucking glorious.

A hot, belligerent look falls over Killian's face. "Don't call that whore my parent. She's a fucking interloper." Quieter, he adds, "Her, and her slut of a daughter."

Jesus fucking wept. If I'm hung up on Genevieve, then how Killian feels about his stepsister, Story, is a whole other level. Rath and I share a long-suffering look. Like me, he's probably remembering the first time Killer called to tell us about her. He was convinced Daniel brought her home for him. I admit, at the time, I was a little jealous. As pissed off as I am about Gen, she was a lot of fucking work as a girlfriend. Things would be so much easier—so much hotter—if my dad would just buy me a pretty little thing to use at will.

But that was before Killian found out about Story's side hustle as a sugar baby.

Before he caught her sitting on his daddy's lap.

"Posey must have a magical pussy if she won your dad over," Rath says, looking vaguely contemplative. "He's got access to as many women as he wants but he picked her. Kind of makes you wonder, right?"

"Jesus Christ, shut the fuck up." Killian scowls and drinks

the last of his beer, tipping the bottle back. To me, he adds, "Rath has a point, Tris. I can call Auggy. She'd come over and set you right. I can add it to Dad's account."

I try to hide my grimace. Augustine is one of Daniel's new whores. She's got legs for days and a nice rack, but the thought of her on her knees doesn't make my dick hard. That's just what Augustine does. There's no power in that. There's no worship. There's no fun. "That's like shooting fish in a barrel. That's not going to make me feel better."

Plus, if the vibes that girl send out are any indication, she'd just be wishing I was Rath the whole time.

Christ, what does a multi-millionaire have to do to get some goddamn loyalty?

"Well," he lifts his empty bottle. "I know what *will* help. Getting you shitfaced. Come on, there's better liquor upstairs."

Rath pauses the video game, gaze rising with ours to the ceiling when more footsteps sound out. "Sure that's not your dad?" Daniel is cool enough, not caring if we drink or fuck around down here, but his temper is almost as legendary as his son's, and I spend most of my time trying not to get on the other side of it.

Killian's eyes follow the sound above us, narrowing as we stand. "The only person here besides us is that little cunt."

"Ah, Sweet Cherry," Rath gives this slow, lazy laugh. "I can't believe she picked that screen name."

"It fits," Killian says, climbing the stairs ahead of us. "I'm pretty sure that cherry is firmly intact. At least for now. She plays a big game with these assholes online, but she still sleeps with a teddy bear, and she only started her period like fifteen months ago." He looks back at us. "And you know no one at school is touching her."

Rath snorts. "Because you made it clear she's kryptonite."

"Something makes me think you don't want anyone else to have a go at her," I add. He wouldn't admit it, but this raging ball of flame in my chest?

He's been feeling it for a year now.

It's not just the betrayal. It's not even the loss of something we felt was ours. It's the fucking rejection that makes it burns so hot.

"*Don't.*" He stops at the top of the stairs and looks down at us. Even knowing he wouldn't ever hurt me or Rath, there's no arguing Killian's an intimidating bastard. He looks past Rath and eyes me. "You know what? You need your dick sucked so bad?" He shrugs, gesturing to the door he swings open. "Go for it."

It takes a minute to follow, but when it clicks, my eyebrows shoot up. "With her? Your stepsister?"

"If she wants to be a whore like her mother, then maybe it's time we started treating her like one." His arms cross over his chest. "You have my permission. Do whatever you want."

Only two things would make me feel better right now; setting something on fire or getting revenge. The suggestion of fucking with Killian's sister doesn't quite fit either of those needs, but something about it still sends a pulse through my veins. It travels down my belly to the dark recesses of my balls.

In the kitchen, Killian nods toward the laundry room, "Now's your chance." I smirk and take a step forward, but he grabs my arm. There's an intensity to his eyes that would make me pause even if he weren't holding me. "If you do this, Mercer, you can't hold back. It's all or nothing."

I spot the hard glint in his eye. There's a reason his nickname is Killer. He's fucking ruthless. We've done a lot of dirty shit in the past, fucked with girls and sent them home crying, but I understand what he's saying. Story isn't Gen. She's no one's girlfriend. This can't be nice or sweet, because all of that was swept off the table a year ago. I wonder if he even realizes that's jealousy in his eyes.

"Understood."

"Good," Rath says, a dark smile curving on his mouth. "Instill a little fear in her. Can't go wrong there."

Fueled on their taunts, I stride across the room. The first thing I see is her ass, round and full, bent over a laundry basket. Rath and I have talked about it before. How cute she is. She's not voluptuous and sexy like her mother—not yet, maybe in a few years. But her ass is really sweet, and her tits are filling in nicely.

I'd be lying if I said her face didn't pop into my thoughts once or twice as I railed Gen.

"Thank god," she sighs, snagging a cotton shirt out of the pile of laundry. "Found you."

"Nope," I say, feeling Rath line up beside me. "Looks like *we* found *you*."

Her eyes widen in surprise and her mouth flops open like a fish. My dick swells at the sight of her lips, all puffy and pink. She definitely didn't hear us coming.

"God, you scared me." She exhales in temporary relief, her eyes darting between us. "You shouldn't sneak around like that."

"Why not?" I ask, flashing a grin. "You're the one sneaking around up here like a frightened little mouse."

Unease settles into her features. Killian's stepsister grew up in a world of sex-workers and johns. There's no doubt she's got a sixth sense for trouble, and from the way her nose wrinkles, she smells it now.

"Check it out," Rath says, jerking his chin at her. "Story's not wearing a bra."

The comment elicits two reactions; her nipples tighten and peak, pushing at the thin cotton of her T-shirt, and her face blooms red. God, it's delicious. The kind of girls we run with are so far beyond blushing, I'd forgotten what it looks like to fluster someone.

"Perky little nipples, eh?" I say, taking a step into the small room. I grip the doorjamb, trapping her inside. Swiping my tongue over my bottom lip, I stare at her tits. "Are they sensitive? Did they get hard just from me talking about them? Or do I need to touch them?"

Her jaw drops and she covers her chest protectively. "You're a pig,' she bites, voice laced in venom. She makes a feeble attempt to get past us but there's no chance. Not unless we let her. This game is getting more fun by the second. She fumes as she realizes we're blocking her. "Get out of my way."

"Answer one question for us, Story, and then we'll let you go," Rath says, propping his shoulder against the jamb. He's wearing a lazy smirk and her nose wrinkles again, probably smelling the beer wafting off him. She pushes up on her toes, trying to look over our shoulders. For what? Help?

It's not coming, sweetheart.

She seems to know it too, because she asks, "What do you want to know?"

Rath toys with the ring on his lip, then asks, "Are you a virgin?"

"What?" Her cheeks turn impossibly redder. "That's none of your business!"

We both laugh and I shake my head. "Oh, *Story*. Only virgins say it's no one's business. You just gave yourself away."

"Well, who cares?" She snaps. "So what? I'm a virgin. Big deal!"

"Nothing we didn't already know," I say, taking another step forward. She moves back and bumps into the hard edge of the washing machine, the shirt in her hands held protectively in front of her. "You have that look. All innocent and clean and pure. The kind of thing that just makes you want to..." I reach out for the soft, pale skin of her collarbone. She bats my hand away and a flicker of dark want snakes up my spine. "Mess it all up."

Rath rakes his bottom lip through his teeth and even I see the shift, he's no longer just fucking around, he's into this. "There's something about virgins, you know?"

"That nervous energy," I agree, eyes fixed to the pulse in her throat. "It gets my dick hard."

"I like the begging." Rath adds, his deep voice shifting into a falsetto, *"Please don't, it hurts!"*

All the color drains from her face, replaced by a pale pallor. It just eggs me on.

"But my favorite part," I say, "is breaking them in. Feeling that tight pussy wrapped around my cock?" I deliberately reach down to...*shift* myself. "There's nothing better than that. Damn, what I'd give to break you in right."

I haven't had a virgin in years.

"You guys are disgusting," she says, lifting my chin. "I'm not scared of you, you know. You're just a bunch of socially-stunted shitheads. That's probably the only way you can get it, isn't it? Bullying girls into giving it up? No wonder your sorry ass got dumped."

There's a short stretch of stillness before the inferno in my chest rages back to life, churning and pulsing.

Fucking bitch.

If this was a game before, just two assholes toying with our best friend's little sister, that's over. Her eyes blaze bright with smug amusement, like she knows exactly how deep her words cut. Well, this little girl just sealed her fate.

"What did you just say to me?"

She shrugs, shifting her attention to Rath. "Guess *someone* in the senior class has more than two brain cells to rub together."

Shit.

It's a well-known secret that Rath struggles academically. I'm not saying he's dumb, because he's not. He's a fucking music prodigy. He can read notes, but the written word isn't his friend. Before he responds, she looks back at me and adds, "It's not like it's a secret that Genevieve tossed you to the curb. Too bad money can't buy you a personality to go with your micro dick."

This little girl is playing with fire, and from the expression on her face, she likes it. She senses what's going to happen a beat too late. I move quickly, darting forward and clamping my hand around her throat. Her chest hitches on a panicked inhale, and her hands grab at my wrists.

She's no match for my strength.

I don't actually squeeze her throat, but I flex my fingers, making it crystal clear. *I could* and I would. Roughly, I say, "Pretty shitty way to treat someone who was just giving you some compliments. Isn't that right, Rath?"

"Rude as fuck," Rath agrees.

"Maybe," I say, prying her fingers from my wrist, "we should show her just how small our dicks *aren't*." I yank her hand down until it's pressed to the bulge at the front of my jeans. "As you so obnoxiously just pointed out, I seem to be finding myself short of a steady fuck these days. Maybe I'll take you, after all."

She fights to pull my hand away, mouth screwing up in disgust, but I hold her palm there for a long moment, grinding against it. Blood pumps to my cock, encouraged both by her fear and the thrill of having an audience. "Fighting will only make it hurt more, baby. I know that's not what you want…or is it?" I tilt my head, assessing her. "Maybe you would, huh? You like it rough? Because we're good with that."

Rath stonily adds, "Crazy good."

She opens her mouth to speak, but nothing comes out. I can see her mind working, racing, as she tries to figure out an escape. With every passing second, she's starting to get it, beginning to understand. This is happening. I can hear it in her voice when she finally speaks.

"Come on, let me go." The tremble in her voice makes me harder. "I just want to go back to my room."

"But the fun's just beginning, isn't it?"

A shadow moves in the doorway and her eyes dart over. I see Killian's broad shoulders taking up the entire space. He looks between the three of us, expression cold.

"Killian," Story says, eyes pleading, "tell them to let me go."

"What's going on?" he asks casually, like I don't have his sister by the throat, pinned to the washing machine. If he asked me to knock it off, I would. But he won't. *This* was his idea. "I thought you were bringing down more beer."

Rath's dark eyes remain fixed on her as he explains, "Story was just telling us how she's a virgin."

Killian hums, like he's bored. "Was she, now?"

I stare at Story. "We were saying how we'd be happy to help her fix that pesky problem."

She swallows and tries again. "Killian, I don't know why you don't like me, but—"

"You don't know why I don't like you?" He barks a caustic, scoffing laugh. "Your white-trash slut of a mother wrecks my family, and brings her little whoreling with her, and you can't figure out why I don't like you." His eyes slither down her body, lip curling. "I don't give a shit what these two do to you. They could both fuck you at the same time, and you know what I'd do?" His eyes finally catch life. "I'd *laugh*."

The look on her face as it hits home, *really* hits home, that Killian isn't going to save her is precious. Absolutely perfection.

"I'll tell your dad," she cries, voice an octave higher. "I'll tell him that you let them do it."

Killian's face hardens. "Just because my dad has some idiotic weakness for sluts doesn't mean he'd choose you over me."

"If you let me go, we can pretend this never happened, okay?" she says, switching tactics. "I won't—I will never say a thing, Killian, I swear."

Abruptly, he barks out a harsh laugh. "You're such a fucking idiot. I really hope your tits get bigger, because that's clearly all you've got going for you. You really think I'd let trash like you live under my roof and not come up with some leverage of my own?"

Her eyes dart wildly between us. "Leverage?"

He reaches into his pocket and pulls out his phone. I tighten my grip on her neck but sweep my thumb over her jaw, stroking little circles into it. Each caress sends a delicious tremor across her limbs. Killian holds up the screen and recognition crosses her features when she sees her sugar baby profile page on display.

"That's right, *Sweet Cherry*. You say a word about me and my friends, and I'll show my idiot dad, who thinks you're the most innocent little snowflake, exactly what you've been doing online." He flips through the photos of Story wearing too little or too tight clothing in a variety of suggestive poses. "Quite the little lucrative business you've got going on, Cherry. You may be a virgin but you're far from innocent. I mean, who's to say anyone would even believe you after seeing this? You, slutting it up just like your gold-digging mother? Tsk tsk." He taps the phone on his chin, eyes full of amusement. "Nah, I think you'll give my boys exactly what they want."

I find it amusing, in a sick sort of way, that she'll never understand what this is really about. Big brother has been going out of his goddamn mind knowing all those old, pervy eyes are taking a piece of what's rightfully his.

"I'll give you a cut of the money," she says, eyes begging. "Whatever I make, I'll give you a quarter. *No*. Half of it!"

Killian laughs darkly. "That's fucking rich. You giving *me* money? You two hearing this shit?"

I smile down at her. "Oh, Sweet Cherry, we don't want your money. I thought we made that clear." I bend and run my nose down her cheek, glancing back at Rath. "How do we want to do this? Who gets to pop this delicious little cherry?"

She tenses and Rath wagers, "You fuckers owe me for last month." Without asking, I know he's talking about the dent we put in the bumper of his jalopy. Killer and I have really nice cars. When the three of us really want to wreak some havoc, we use Rath's.

I shake my head. "Eat shit, that's nowhere near equal value. You still owe me for Sophomore year." I'd never throw money up in Rath's face, but the girl he stole right out from under my nose—pre-Genevieve? Well, who fucking knows? Maybe if I'd gotten a taste of her pussy, I wouldn't have bothered with Gen.

"You're still on about that?" Rath complains, face hardening. "Fine. Three thousand and my guitar."

He doesn't really have that money, but Story doesn't know that. She quakes at the negotiations, the nail hammering harder and harder into her coffin.

"Please don't do this," she begs. "Don't hurt me. I'll give you whatever you want, just don't...take *that*."

"Ah, the begging," Rath groans, hand coming down to cup his crotch. "Fine, four thousand."

Story buckles and I shift my hands to hold her up. Rath slides behind her, fingers cinching around her waist. She looks to Killian one last time, silently pleading with him, but predictably, his gaze is cold. Uncaring. It's more than obvious he doesn't give a damn about what happens to her.

That's why it shocks me when he says, "Neither of you are fucking her." I guess he finally sees the flare of possessive jealousy in his eyes for what it actually is. That's fair. She's his by rights. "Do whatever else you want to, I don't care, but..." He rakes his fingers through his hair, looking away, jaw tight. "The last thing I need is for her to bleed out all over the laundry room floor. I'm not cleaning that shit up, and I'm sure as hell not explaining it to my dad."

Yeah, sure.

That's why he doesn't want anyone else's dick breaking her

in.

Rath mutters a curse of disappointment, but even though I didn't come here to fuck her, she doesn't need to know that. I take a step back and sweep my eyes over her. "Fine. Let's see your tits."

She hesitates but Rath is tired of waiting, he grabs the straps of her tank top and shoves them down her arms. Her tits spring out, perfect and round. Nipples dark pink and pebbled into hard points. Rath grunts behind her, looking up at me with a smirk. I lick my lips and reach for her, grazing the underside. "A little small, but soft. Am I the first one to touch them?"

Story has the tits of a woman who doesn't quite know how to use them yet. They're supple and fresh-looking, nice and perky.

She clamps her mouth shut. Defiant. I like it. I grin and pinch her nipple, eliciting a yelp. She squirms and tries to twist away, but Rath doesn't let her, holding her tight. She recoils when she feels his boner.

"I asked you a question, Sweet Cherry." I continue toying with her nipple, being more gentle now.

"Yes," She grinds out. "You're the first."

"Thank you." I tweak her softly and she squirms.

"Dude," Killian says from the doorway, "I know you're having a bad week and working some shit out here, but my dad will be home soon. Whatever you're going to do, just get on with it."

The mention of Gen makes the fire in my chest hum to life. It wants to burn. It wants to *consume*. I run my thumb over my mouth pretending to think, but we all know where this is going. Well, maybe everyone but her.

"Get on your knees."

With Killian's warning, I don't waste my time, unbuckling my belt and yanking down my jeans. I'm in a commando phase, because I read that letting your junk breathe is good for your sperm. Her eyes widen when she's confronted with my dick. I'm hard, the skin straining over the tautness. She stares, probably awed by the gloriousness of seeing a Mercer dick, frozen until Rath pushes her down on her knees.

He goes down with her, chest and hips pressed against her backside. I see him lower his zipper with one hand while the other kneads her tit.

"What are you doing?" she asks him, even though her wide, horrified eyes never leave my cock.

"Watching," he says, biting her earlobe. "Feeling. Getting off. There's more than one way to enjoy a girl."

She rips her eyes away from my dick to stare at Killian, but what she sees makes her face go slack in terror. He's shoving his hand down his pants, pulling out his own cock. I raise an eyebrow and he shrugs. There was no way he'd opt out of this one. He may not touch her, but he's going to enjoy the fuck out of this. He leans back against the door jamb and takes two long strokes as he watches.

Dude can even make jerking off look intimidating.

I face her again, touching her under the chin, redirecting her gaze at my face. "Open up, Sweet Cherry. I want your eyes on me the whole time. I want to see those pretty lips wrapped around my cock. I want to see it when I come, and you swallow it down. I want you to watch me while it happens." A straining ache fills my balls and I thumb her pretty mouth open. "Understood?"

She nods, the fight drained out of her. She opens her mouth and I feel the slick, warm heat engulf me. I groan at the feel of her, fisting my hand in her hair. Fuck, I haven't felt a girl's mouth around my dick in at least a year. Her eyes close and the sound of Rath's breathing rattles through the air. I watch as he plucks at her nipples, sweeping his hand down her belly.

Story fumbles through the blow job, clumsy and inexperienced. I prod at her cheek and ask, "Never sucked a dick before, have you, Cherry?" Still feels good, though. I just can't help but have a little fun. "You realize that's where the real money is, don't you? Daddies would pay a sweet penny for some head if you can do it right."

Sick of holding back, I tighten my grip and thrust hard against the back of her throat.

With her eyes closed, she sputters, choking, gasping for air, and it makes my belly clench in arousal.

I hold her still, trying to keep my voice low and threatening.

"I thought I told you to look at me. Not very good at following instructions, are you?"

Reluctantly, her eyes open and shift back to my face.

"That's a girl," I say, patting her head like a dog. "I'll make this easy on you."

It's a lie. I'm a liar. I thrust hard and painful into her mouth. Her hands reach out, grappling at my hips to slow me down, but I don't stop. I give a few sharp thrusts against the back of her throat, reveling in the wet, choking sound she makes.

"Either I fuck your mouth, or you get better at this. Your choice, Story."

She holds my hips and glares up at me. Her eyes glisten with tears, but my cock thickens at the fire I see in them. Every sign of weakness, every vulnerability, makes me that much harder, and I know she can feel it on her tongue. I thrust in, and she falls in line, angry and bitter. I don't give a fuck. I'm not here for love and respect. I'm here to get me some.

"Fuck," I mutter, my jaw slackening. "Yeah, that's it. Shit, she's really doing it."

I've really missed blow jobs. The sight of a girl on her knees, gazing up at me. The feel of their tongue as they struggle to take all of me to the hilt. The look in their eyes when I make them. It's a battle not to grip her head and just fuck her throat anyway. I'm not sure how Killer would take it, though.

Rath jerks himself off while his hand travels down her flat

stomach, shoving it into the waistband of her thin shorts. She doesn't even fight.

I can't hear what he's whispering into her ear, but her fingers dig so deep into my hips she's going to cause bruising. Bring it, sweetheart.

Whatever he says makes her tears spill over, leaving hot tracks down her cheeks. I bring my hand to her cheek and thumb them away. "Don't cry, now. We're just having a good time. You want us to have a good time, don't you?" She continues sucking but doesn't look appreciative of my kind words. "I don't get it, Killer," I say, glancing over at him. "Used to be, we could show a girl a little attention and she'd trip over her own feet to be ours. Nowadays, all these bitches do is fuck around."

The image of Genevieve fucking that goddamn softball coach fills my mind. It isn't that she's a slut. Most girls are. It's that she's so fucking *stupid* for throwing me away. As if I'm not good enough. As if she has the fucking *right* to reject *me*.

I fist Story's hair, yanking her deeper onto my dick. It makes her cry harder, these sweet little hitched sobs against the head of my dick. Those are what make me shudder.

My head falls back and I close my eyes as the orgasm rips through me. My cock twitches, dumping cum against her tongue. I cup the back of her head and press her close, holding her still as I empty myself between her lips.

Behind her, Rath grunts, yanking her back against his chest, and she's caught in the middle of us, being pulled two different ways. Killer's breathless groan fills the room as he busts his own nut.

I pull out of her mouth, but not before I grab her hair again and rasps out, "You know what to do now, don't you?"

Rath yanks hands out of her shorts and the scent of her pussy fills the air. He grips her chin with wet fingers and commands, "Swallow him down, pretty girl."

It takes her more than one try to do it without gagging, but I'll give it to her. She holds my gaze and obeys, swallowing every drop, throat jumping with the motion.

"Good," I say, stroking her cheek in approval. "You're so good for us, aren't you, Cherry?"

She stumbles to her feet, legs wobbly, skin pale. Rushing from the room, her hand clamps around her mouth like she's about to puke. Killian lets her pass and the three of us laugh as her footsteps echo across the kitchen. In a minute, she'll be safe upstairs, locked in her room.

But the three of us will be down here, talking about how much we want another go.

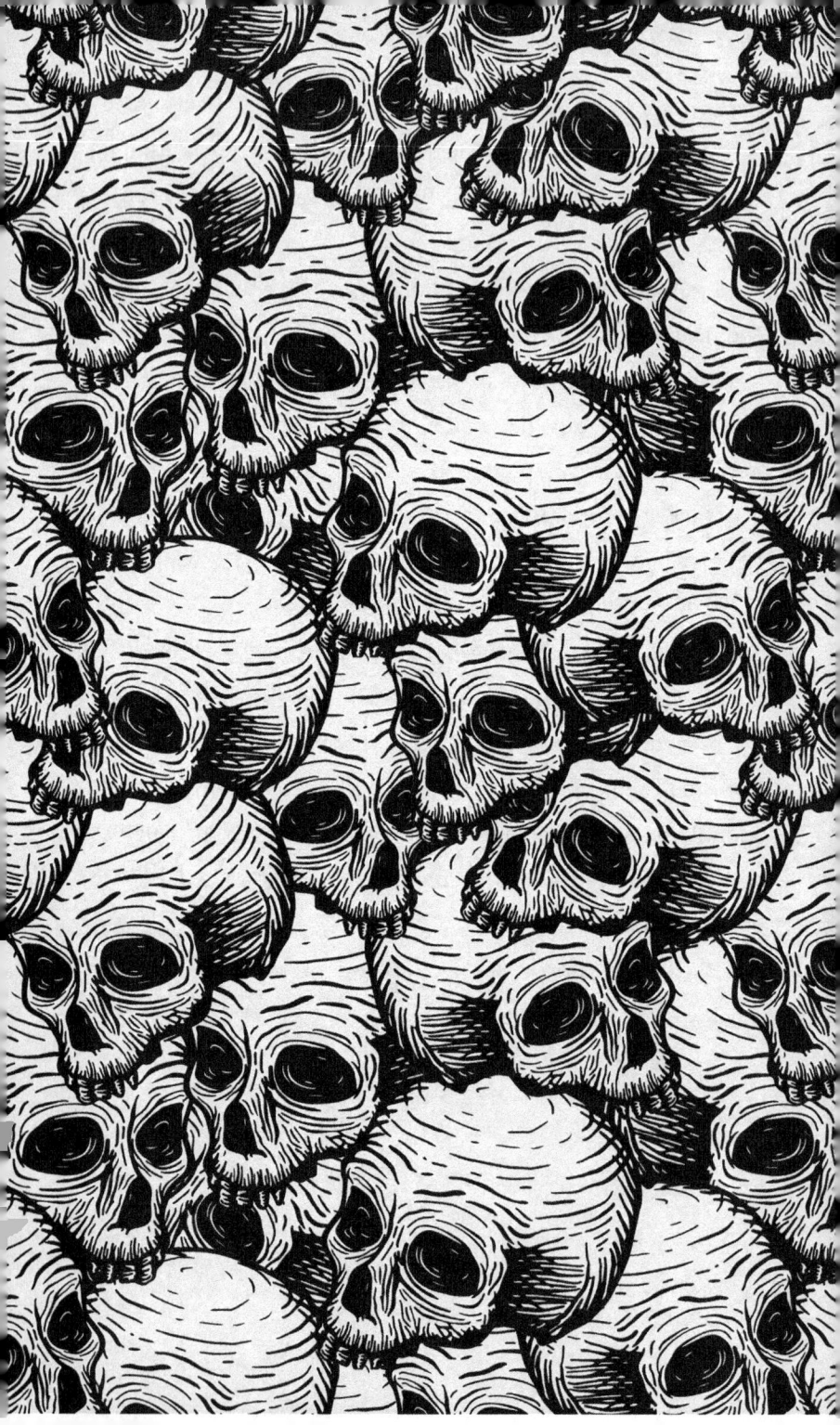

DIMITRI
RATHBONE

2

MOVING

"SWALLOW HIM DOWN, pretty girl." I stare at her red mouth, slick with spit and Tristian's come, and I won't even lie. I wish it were me. She forces it back, managing not to gag on his spunk, eyes darting between the two of us. They're red and wet, but those tears mean nothing here. Tristian strokes her cheek and praises her, finally releasing her. Dark laughter bubbles from the three of us as she runs. I look at Killian to make sure he's really okay with this, but he's just grimacing down at the mess of cum on the floor.

"Jesus," he says, "next time I'm coming in her, too. This is a fucking mess."

No regrets then.

It's a surprise. I figured Tristian would share Gen with us before Killer ever shared his sister, but here we are, all cumbrained in the laundry room as Story stomps her way up the stairs.

While the boys clean up, I grab a shirt out of the clean laundry basket and wipe off my cock with it. Killian's right. From now on, that spunk goes in—or at the very least *on*—the girl. *Heh.*

"What are you laughing at?" Tristian asks. It's a relief to see some of that tension has drained from his face. I can't fucking stand the thought of him all wounded over that fucking bitch.

"Just thinking about how fun it would be to fuck with her a little more." I'm definitely planning on this happening again. At school. In the janitor's closet. In the music room. Why not? I haven't come that hard in a long time—by my hand or someone else's.

"What do you think, Killer?" Tristian asks, stuffing himself back into his pants. "Maybe we should have a regular playdate with Sweet Cherry." His smile is all wicked, but I see the careful thing lurking in his eyes. He's testing the waters here.

"You're drunk," Killian tells him. Then, he looks at me. "And you're a pervert."

That didn't sound like a *no.*

I toss the dirty shirt into the washer, but when I turn, I notice something stuck to the side of the basket. A pair of pale pink panties with little flowers stitched on the side. I zip myself back into my jeans and shove the panties in my pocket.

Killian kicks us out a little while later, warning me not to let Tristian set any fires. When we were kids, we could get away with super petty shit. Dumb stuff. Reckless, destructive vandalism was never above us, back then. But now that we're older, Daniel is watching us more and more. He has big plans for the three of us—first Forsyth, then pledging LDZ, then taking over as Lords. I don't even know what all that shit means, unlike Tristian and Killian who are both legacies. But I do know it involves parties, power, and a fuck-ton of pussy. Who would say no to that? It's not like my future's exactly bright, anyway.

"Did you hear those little cries she made?" Tristian says as I drive across town. The ambush worked. He seems to have forgotten about Genevieve betraying him for at least a few minutes. Now, he just wants to relive the scene in the laundry room all over again. "She was dying for it."

"She's a whore, just like her mother," I say, jerkily changing gears. The transmission in my piece-of-shit beater is going to fall out any day now. "You can't trust girls like that." He probably thinks I'm talking about hustlers, which…true. But mostly I just mean people like me. People who come from rough beginnings and rougher middles. People who are desperate.

"Hey," he says, voice seeming half distracted. "Turn right up here." He jerks his chin, but his eyes are glued to his phone. Deceptively casual. That's our Tris.

"How stupid do you think I am?" I step on the gas, speeding past the turn off to Genevieve's house. "You'll get your shot in, but not like this. You're a fucking live wire."

He slides me a cold, disappointed look, but drops it.

I'm still stuck on Sweet Cherry. The way her body felt against mine, the sticky slick heat between her legs, the way her mouth looked taking his cock. I'm getting hard just thinking about it again. Because the thing is, I doubt she is a whore. There's zero experience there. No finesse. No acting. Story Austin is just a sweet little lamb, ripe for the slaughter.

My dick twitches at the thought of us getting there first.

I pull up in front of Tristian's massive house. He climbs out, but sticks his head back in the open door before shutting it.

"That was fun," he says, as though he's not talking about us assaulting our best friend's sister. "Getting me out of my head and everything. Thanks for..." He taps the hood of the car and looks away, like he's having trouble finding the words.

I don't make him struggle. "No problem, brother," I say, glad I stopped him from acting too rash. That bitch is going to pay. Not tonight, but soon. I have no doubt about that.

He blows out a hard breath, nodding. "Sure you don't want to stay over? I've got more liquor. I can call some people over."

I spend the night a lot—either here or at Killian's. Their houses are a hell of a lot more comfortable than my own. Quiet. Clean. Sometimes I just want to get away from the oppressive loneliness of my place. But I'm not feeling it tonight. I've got a wild energy running through me and the urge to get home. "Nah. I'll see you tomorrow."

"Yup." He nods, giving the hood another tap before stepping back. "Night."

He slams the door and lopes up the front steps, falling once against the railing. The door to Mercer Manor is huge, like the mansion has some malevolent, gaping jaw. A moment later, Tristian vanishes inside.

The entire drive to my apartment, I feel the urge to turn around, go back to Killer's and find his little sister. I'd sneak in the backdoor using the code for the touchpad lock and sneak up to her room. Then I'd take my time with her, getting her wet again and popping that cherry for real.

I resist, hands clenched around the steering wheel, and head across town, deep to the center of South Side. I crank up the bass on my stereo until I feel the music more than hear it. The beat matches the adrenaline pumping in my veins and I cling to that feeling long after I've parked and found a spot on the road.

Unfortunately, the second I step out, I'm approached by one of the Avenue regulars.

Augustine. "Hey, Rath!" She's chewing on a piece of gum, jaw working up and down.

I give her a smile that I can only hope doesn't look like a grimace. "Hey."

"You're out late," she says, leaning against the light post. She pops her hip out, drawing attention to her bare midriff. It's not often Mr. Crane makes them work this side of the Avenue.

Business must be slow. "You have a party or something?"

I don't look Auggy in the eye. I sort of can't stand her. It's not that she's a bitch or anything, she's just depressing as all shit. "Something like that," I reply, gesturing to the decrepit rowhouse behind her. Probably not a coincidence she's on this particular corner. "Gotta get to bed. Early day tomorrow."

Her face falls, but she works hard to catch it. That's what Auggy does. Works hard. Even that little move she just made, popping her hips out, all 'come hither'...

"Bummer," she says, eyes never leaving my face. "I was thinking we could go out some time. You and me? There's a show tomorrow night. That punk bar out by the river?"

Augustine works *too* hard.

I weigh my keys in my hands, and it's the strangest thing. I've got a legitimate hooker standing in front of me, tits hanging out, stomach completely bare, legs covered in ripped up fishnets, offering to take me to what's probably going to be a really good punk show. But all I can think about is Story on that laundry room floor, fumbling and terrified. Shaking my head, I say, "I don't think so, Augustine," and I leave her there, staring after me.

Probably a dick move, but the girl can't take a hint.

I climb the three floors to my apartment, slotting the key into the lock. It's dark inside. Mom's working the late shift. I open the refrigerator and find a plate covered in foil. Mom's not around much but she makes sure I eat. She worries I'm too skinny to run the streets for Daniel, so she's always trying to bulk me up. She doesn't know that I don't want to get stuck in South Side, that I want to play music. It's a dream I can chase, but I know I'll never catch it. Why break her heart as well as mine?

The pizza and beer are still sit heavy in my stomach, so I save the food for later. I go into my room and flick on the lights before I shut the door. My brother, Alessio, and I used to share a room until he turned eighteen and enlisted, fucking off to parts unknown. That was eight years and ten apartments ago, though. Mom and I are constantly dipping from place to place, depending on various factors, such as the cost of rent, the proximity to her work, the shittiness of the neighbors. Sometimes we duck out in the middle of the night, sneaking past the super's door. Always gotta be ready to bounce. Everything I own can fit into two trash bags. I keep the good shit, like the keyboard and sound equipment Tristian bought for me, at one of their places.

Mercers haven't moved since the 1800s or something.

My room—or this year's version of it—is a jumbled mess of dirty clothes, sheet music, and half-fixed instruments I've dragged out of dumpsters. Beside the bed, a bong is nestled up next to my shoes. I shove the schoolwork off my bed, ignoring the 'F' at the top of my English paper and shuck off my shirt. I clamp my headphones over my ears and turn on something old, classical. I like the rise and fall of the masters. Bach, Beethoven,

Debussy. Their music sounds like the words of Gods. I turn off the lights and climb into bed, but even with the music, I still can't settle.

My mind and body are both still too focused on Sweet Cherry. The smell of her hair. The tremble of fear running through her body. I've intimated girls before, pushed them past questionable consent. I've gotten off to tears and humiliation, to the pleading glint in their eye, but nothing came as close as this. *Pure ecstasy.* I've never been that hard before and I've stayed hard ever since.

I reach for the bong and quickly pack the bowl. The spark of the lighter and two deep inhalations later, I feel the smooth release traveling through my system and finally, some of the tension. My mind wanders and I remember the souvenir I'd stashed in my pocket. Pulling them from my jeans pocket, I press them against my nose, inhaling the clean laundry scent, and wishing it smelled like her pussy instead.

Will she notice they're gone? Is she lying in her bed behind a locked door? Is she crying? Is she telling her mom? Is she feeling ashamed and wanting more?

The thoughts tug at the base of my balls, sending a flare to the pit of my stomach. I pull out my cock and run the smooth fabric of her panties against the hard, hot flesh. Leaning back, I fondle the cotton over my balls, eliciting a low building ache that spreads through my pelvis. "Jesus," I mutter to myself, surprised at the ferocity of my horniness. I'd just blown my nut an hour ago, but the panties and memory of Sweet Cherry bring it all back with a vengeance. I stroke and glide my hand over my cock, forcing myself to take my time. The vividness of the memory is sure to fade, and I want to savor it as long as possible. I hook the panties around my cock and pull, feeling the stretch. My fingers roll over the tip and my belly dips, sending a spiral of want back down to my balls. *Tug and push.* The coil turns and tightens. *Push and tug.* I close my eyes and think of how tight her pussy must be. She plays up the slutty sugar baby thing, but the virginity is obvious. She likes to play games. Well, baby, so do I.

The game we'd play would be dangerous. Delicious. She'd beg me not to do it, cry that she's saving herself. I'd laugh in her face and roughly spread her legs. I'd take my time, but not in a gentle way. Just to make it last longer. To get the most out of it. To feel her sheathed around me until I couldn't take it anymore.

Motherfucker, she'd bleed.

She'd bleed on my cock as I fucked her, and she'd beg. Not for me to stop. She'd beg for me to let her come, to rub that slick blood over her clit until she tightened around me, screaming.

In the pale light of my room, my eyes jolt open when the groan and orgasm rip through me at the same time. Over the rise and fall of my fist, I watch the slippery spunk slide down my fist in ropey spurts. I catch what I can in her panties, wiping up the mess on my hand. The sticky-wetness seeps through the cotton but I roll it up tight, not wanting to lose a drop.

Just having my cum on something that belongs to her is enough to settle the electricity in my veins.

For now.

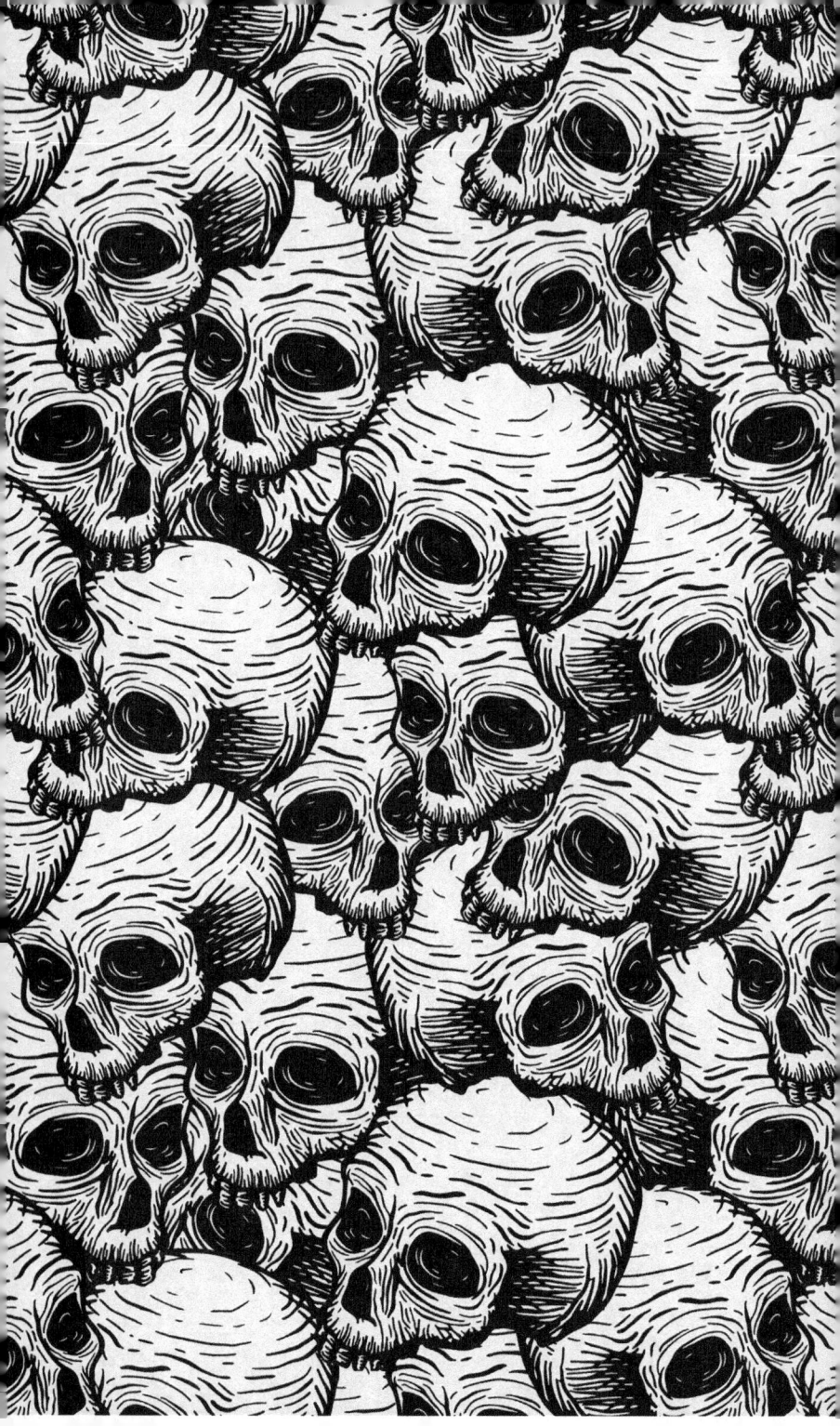

3

SLIPPING

WHAT DO YOU say after your best friend mouth-raped your stepsister and you watched? Not much. We laughed after Story ran upstairs, eyes filled with horror. That little bitch got what she deserved, though, always prancing around the house in those little tanks and booty shorts. It'd been a gut punch when I found her sugar baby profile. Even worse when I saw the old perverts nickle and diming her with gift cards and app payments.

I would have given her so much more.

"She was hot for it," Rath says after he emerges from the laundry room, cleaned up. Tristian had gotten off easy, literally. He shot his load in her mouth while the two of us had to clean up a mess. He fishes his keys out of his pocket. "Her pussy was soaked."

"Bullshit," I say, not sure if I believe it. "She was crying."

He shrugs in that loose, cocky way that drives girls like

Augustine crazy. "Some chicks like a little pain with their pleasure. You know that."

Maybe it drives girls like Story crazy, too.

I shouldn't be surprised. I knew she was a whore. I'm just pissed she derived any pleasure from Tristian choking her with his cock. She should feel pain and humiliation. Nothing more.

"I'm taking him home," Rath says, pushing Tristian toward the door. Tris downed two glasses of rum after Story ran upstairs, so he's drunk as hell.

"Make sure he doesn't set any fires on the way," I warn.

Rath laughs, but we both know it's not a joke. From the glint in his eye, I'm not convinced he'll keep our pyro from setting Genevieve's house on fire, but I'm ready for them to go. I'm not quite done with little sister yet.

When I'm sure they're gone, I close up downstairs, shutting off the lights and locking the backdoor. Dad and Posey are at a charity event, but if it looks quiet, they'll go straight to bed, assuming Story and I are tucked away in our rooms. They're half right. Story goes to bed like clockwork, crawling into bed and watching videos on her phone until she falls asleep. I briefly wonder if she's upstairs crying about what happened in the laundry room or if Rath's right, that she liked it and wants more. The thought sends a thrill down my spine.

Upstairs, I stand outside her room for a long moment, ear pressed against the door. Her light is off and I can't hear the sound of her computer or phone. I try the knob and it's locked. I've often wondered why she locks the door. Is it to keep my dad out? Me? A habit from back when her mother was hooking?

I'm not bothered, entering my room next door, and opening the bathroom that connects our room. For some reason, little sister never thinks to lock *this* door. Foolish girl. My cock twitches, anticipation building as I carefully push it open. The crack of light sweeps across the foot of her bed. She's curled on her side—eyes closed.

Waiting for me.

I step inside quickly, closing the door behind me. It takes a moment for my eyes to adjust, but I know this path like the back of my hand. Four strides to the end of the bed. Two more to stand next to her. I do it quickly—silently—using the speed and balance that makes me a winner on the football field. When I'm in the right spot, where the sliver of light from outside the window bathes her lower part of her face, I focus on her mouth—tonight more than ever. Before, it was just a fantasy that ran through my mind a million times, but now I know what she looks like with her pink lips wrapped around a thick cock. The way her eyes widened when he pushed in deep, making her gag. The wince of pain when Tristian grabbed the back of her neck, her hair, and pulled her close. Jesus, the image is burned into my eyes and my balls twitch at the memory.

I was joking when I suggested it to Tristian, but the second it was out there, I couldn't take it back. That fucker has been dying to get his hands on Story for months. The breakup and booze, the hate pumping through his veins, created a perfect storm, and Story Austin was the trailer park in the path of a tornado.

The kind that leaves complete and total annihilation.

In the faint light, I can see her lips are still swollen and red, abused from Tristian fucking her mouth. He was brutal. Mean. Punishing. And Rath, that bastard had his hands all over her. All over what belonged to me. I don't resent *them* for it. We take what we want, but I won't deny I'm jealous. My goddamn father screwed me out of this girl. She was supposed to be mine, but he's too greedy to share. That's the real reason I let Tristian take her.

Ruin her for my father.

Make her yours.

Make her ours.

Make her anything but *his*.

I stare at her face, at the long eyelashes, full cheeks, and pointed nose. When I walked in the laundry room, she looked at me with relief—*hope*. Stupid slut. Even though I was jealous, I still got hard. I pulled out my cock and jerked off right there, in front of my best friends, all to humiliate my stepsister. The look of horror fueled my erection. Those tears, the pleading— goddamn, it was hot. Rejecting her was even better. She needed to know what she was to me. Trash. Garbage. Nothing but a living cum dumpster.

Witnessing that moment was one thing, but seeing her now, sleeping and vulnerable... that ignites a fire in my veins. She's quiet. Innocent. Completely unaware. I push my hand down my shorts and think about taking her like this; pushing my cock between her lips, or yanking those barely-there panties aside and burying myself in her tight, virgin pussy. I stroke the length of my pulsing cock as it gets harder with every glide of my hand. I step closer, pulling it out just enough that, if she woke up, it would be the first thing she saw. Pre-cum builds at the tip and all I want is to rub it over those fleshy lips, marking her as *mine.*

So that's what I do.

It's not the first time, and it won't be the last.

I tip forward, splaying my palm against the wall to hold my weight as I press my knee into the bed, carefully guiding the head of my cock to her mouth. It's not what I really want. In a perfect world, she'd be the one coming to *my* bed. She'd sink her mouth down around my cock without even needing to be asked. She'd look up my body with those big eyes as she sucked me, and she wouldn't be able to talk, but I'd still be able to hear the message in her gaze.

I'm yours, big brother.

Clenching my teeth, I bump my cock right up against the part of her mouth, watching as the light catches my pre-cum, slathered onto her lips. I'm usually more careful than this,

47

but tonight, I just can't help it. There are still pale tracks on her cheeks from her tears, and her eye lashes are all dried and matted. I imagine her crying—begging me—fucking pleading for me to let her be mine. Mine and no one else's.

I shoot my nut right onto her lips.

It's a fucking pathetic load. I'd almost milked my balls dry with that scene in the laundry room earlier. It makes it easy, though. Easy to rub it around without worrying about the mess. Easy to nudge it into her mouth. Easy to pull back and catch the rest with the tips of my fingers, forcing it past her teeth.

I slip back out the way I came, through the adjoining bathroom. Stripping off my shorts, I toss them in the hamper on top. I wash my hands, and look up, getting a glimpse of my face in the mirror. My cheeks are red, pupils blown. A thin layer of sweat covers my brow.

"Killian? You in there?" my dad's voice calls through the closed door.

"One second," I reply. It takes a moment to shift gears, grabbing a semi-clean pair of shorts out of the hamper and pulling them on. I swing open the door and stride into my bedroom, shirtless, avoiding his eyes. I still feel them on me as I pull back the covers, wondering, "What's up?"

"Just checking on you before bed." His tie is loose and I smell the liquor on his breath, even halfway across the room. "Everything go okay tonight?"

I stop, turning to look at him. "Why wouldn't it?"

He holds my stare. "I saw Genevieve's parent's at the fundraiser."

Ah, *the breakup*. He heard. "Tristian just needs to blow off some steam. He'll be fine."

My father knows everything about Rath and Tristian. It's part of being in Daniel Payne's world. My pulse quickens as I wonder… does he know what I was doing in Story's room?

"I get that," he says, "but I don't want any *blow* back in our direction. That's a risk I can't take."

Our eyes lock across the room and the hairs prickle on the back of my neck. I wait for it—for him to tell me that he knows what happened in the laundry room, or that he somehow saw me jerking off standing over Story's innocent, sleeping body.

But he doesn't.

"Tristian's cool. I'm not worried about it."

He holds my eye for a beat longer and steps toward the door. "Good. I'm holding you to that."

He exits the room and shuts the door, leaving me alone. I climb into bed thinking of the girl in the next room. Wondering what happens next. We didn't pop her cherry but we crossed a line. One I doubt any of us can come back from.

LADY

OF

FORSYTH

WE *KEEP*
WHAT'S *OURS*

SAMANTHA RUE
ANGEL LAWSON

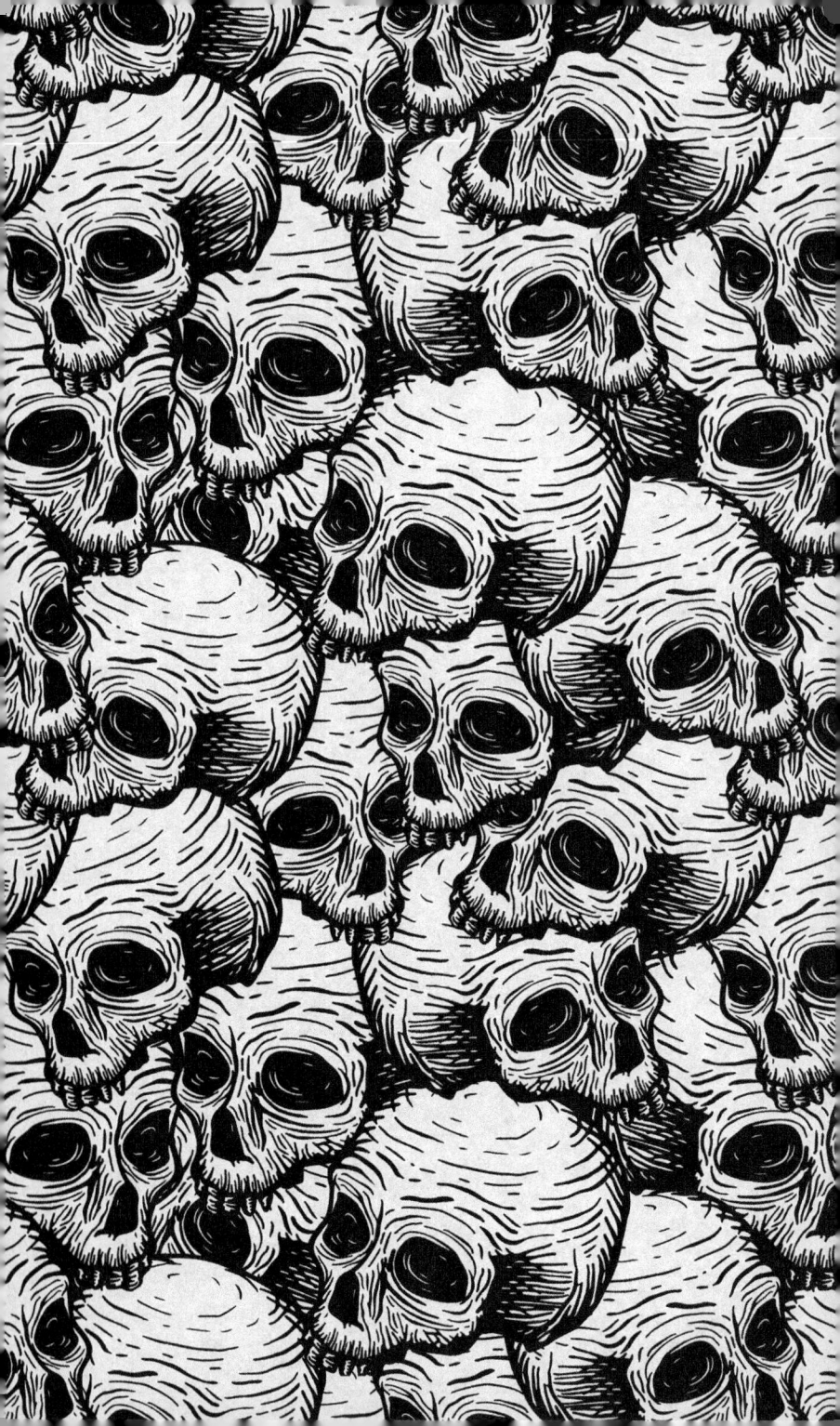

KILLIAN
PAYNE

FEBRUARY

"Mr. Payne, sir," the manager is saying, red-faced and urgent. He's older, about the age my father might be, and looks about three seconds from shitting himself. "We didn't realize the reservation was for you. Please accept my apologies. This section isn't suitable for someone of your standing. If you'll follow me, I'll show you to our very best table."

Story shifts uncomfortably at my side, tossing me a grimace, but I'm too busy scoping out the restaurant for any threats. It's a risk to bring her here, but North Side has the best dining in Forsyth.

Fucking right I didn't put the reservation in my real name.

We're conspicuous. I'm in a nice suit, but there's no hiding my tattoos or the gun bulging in my waistband. Story looks every inch my opposite in a pristine cream-colored dress, lacy and intricate but meant to be worn, cotton beneath all the ornamentation. At first glance, she's the picture of royal purity, but the neckline scoops low.

My initial and half of Tristian's are plainly on display.

"Alright then," I say, nodding as the man turns to lead us to the back. Probably somewhere 'cozy and private', which is doublespeak for 'dark and secluded'.

When I cast a glance at my date, Story's got this shyly impressed look on her face. I guess on the surface, this probably seems like a really generous benefit of being who we are, walking into a five-star restaurant and being immediately fussed over.

But I know the truth.

No North Side establishment will stay one very long if they're seen catering to the likes of South Side's King and Queen.

"Here," the manager says when we arrive. I'll give him this. It definitely has the ambiance. If it weren't for the bead of sweat running down his temple, I could almost pretend giving my Lady and I the very best dining experience possible is actually his top priority.

I slip him a hundred. "We'll start with your finest bottle of wine."

He doesn't even look at the bill, sputtering, "Yes, sir, right away," and then scampers off.

"If that guy has his way," I tell Story, pulling out her chair, "this'll be the quickest dinner you've ever eaten."

She tilts her head, wondering, "What do you mean?"

I wave it off, taking my seat. "I hear their foie gras is the best dish in Forsyth."

"Oh?" She arches an eyebrow. "And who did you hear that from?"

"Sy."

Her loud bark of laughter startles me. "God, do you think he brings Lav here? Could you imagine?"

I try to, but shake my head. Despite her upbringing, the rough and tumble diners of West End seem to suit Lavinia Lucia's personality more than fine dining. Plus, "I think it'd take a lot more than French cuisine to get the Duchess to step foot in North Side again."

The bread and cheese arrives first, followed shortly by a bottle of wine that probably costs as much as Tristian's shoes.

That's saying something.

Money isn't an object. Not that it ever had been, but my father held the purse strings. When Posey killed him, everything came to me. The accounts, the property, the business holdings. My father was a complete and utter piece of shit, but he was good at making money. At first, I felt uncomfortable touching it, but I work my ass off for South Side. I earned it, along with Rath, Tris and Story. So fuck yeah, bring out the most expensive wine. My Lady deserves the best.

My knee keeps jittering, and I feel too large for the chair, tucking my limbs in close. The table is microscopic, my knees snuggled up against hers beneath it. The feeling of being too hemmed in makes me shifty, like there's not enough room to fit into my own skin.

Mistaking this for nervousness, Story's palm covers my hand, my tattooed knuckles pulled tight into a fist against the tabletop. "Hey. It's fine," she assures me, eyes soft and patient. "Even Lav says the Counts are dust. I trust her."

It's a problem.

Story's been getting closer with some of the other Royal women, and sure, the Duchess seems legit. But bitches around here aren't loyal. Trust? Story's use of that word alone tells me she's not watching her back enough. I like the Dukes. I'd back them up if need be. But I wouldn't trust them to have my six, and they wouldn't trust me, either.

I try to shake off the unease, because she's got it all wrong. "I'm not worried about the Counts. I wouldn't have brought you here if I thought it was a risk." Lionel and Perez are dead. Lars ran to Northridge with his tail between his legs. There's no heir to take the crown. I'm nowhere near being North Side's biggest problem.

There's nothing worse for a territory than a kingdom without a King.

No, I'm not nervous.

I'm hard as fucking nails.

That dress of hers is killing me. The way the bodice shifts when she twirls a lock of hair around her forefinger. The feel of her thigh against mine, knowing hers is bare and soft. The way her skin seems to glow against the cream. It's not just the dress, either. Her hair is effortlessly wavy, cheeks a slight pink.

She looks so goddamn innocent.

It's taking every ounce of my self-control to not defile her right here on this table.

"Mrs. Crane asked me to take her on a few errands the other day." She says this nonchalantly as if that comment didn't just shift the world on its axis.

"And... you took her?" Delores doesn't ask anyone to do anything. Other than maybe to kiss her ass.

"Yes, and before you go ballistic, Marcus went with us." The thing about Marcus is I'm pretty sure he's more loyal to Story than he is to me. It's not a problem. The Lady needs some muscle willing to take a bullet for her, but he's also willing to go along with her on these excursions. Still, my shoulders ease a little bit at that information, but there must still be an incredulous expression on my face. "Hey, I was surprised she asked me too."

"Exactly what kind of errands were these?"

"The dry cleaners, the pharmacy to pick up a prescription..." She ticks them off her fingers one by one. "Did you know she's on a statin now? We need to keep an eye on her cholesterol." I raise my eyebrows as she continues, "...the florist, and then the cemetery."

"The cemetery?" That's no man's land. "Babe, you can't just go wandering around–"

She gives me a look. "She wanted to put flowers on her husband's grave. It was their anniversary or something." Her hand squeezes my knee. "It was fine. Sweet."

I narrow my eyes. I don't know how much Story knows about Mr. Crane but nothing Delores has ever done for him, dead or alive, is sweet. "She left a little card tucked behind the flowers. I guess she needed to say some things."

Jesus Christ.

"Did anyone see you?"

She shakes her head. "No. Marcus circled around three times before we finally got out of the car."

"Look, I appreciate you for looking out for her," I say, meaning it. That woman is the closest thing I have to a meddling grandmother. "Just... remember she's not a sweet old lady. She's ruthless. And there's a reason she asked you and not me or Rath."

She'd slit her own wrists before asking Tristian for a favor.

Story rolls her eyes. "It was a message to someone, Killian. Not a letter to the dead. I know that. Why do you think I'm telling you?"

Fuck. This woman. So smart. So sexy and beautiful. Talk about ruthless.

"I'll look into it," I tell her. I go to grab my glass of wine and my hand clumsily knocks it over.

"Fuck!" I try to keep the curse under my breath, but I can feel the tendon in my temple pulsing as I watch the wine splash right into Story's chest. She gasps, flinching back as I lurch forward to catch the stem of the glass, but it's too late.

Her dress–the pristine, pure, innocent cream–blooms with the grisly crimson stain.

Slamming the glass down, I explode, "Why are these fucking tables so fucking small?!"

Story snatches the white linen napkin from her lap and begins frantically dabbing at the stain. "Calm down!" I can't tell if her sharp frown is for me or the dress. "Ugh, now I'm all sticky." She meets my gaze, giving me an exasperated look. "Can I trust your tantrum to wait until I get back from the lady's room?"

I take a deep breath, cracking my neck to hold back the anger coursing through my veins. "I'm fine," I gnash out. And then, "Sorry."

Her hand finds mine again, soothing it flat from my tightly clenched fist. "It won't ruin the night if you don't let it, big brother." Her smile, all gentle and wry, turns knowing as the rage melts away from my expression, and I know just what she's seeing. My eyes are probably fully dilated as they dip down to her cleavage. I'm pretty sure she could call me 'big brother' and make me forget my own fucking name.

"I won't," I promise, watching as she leaves her seat and heads for the bathroom.

The second she's out of sight, I burst into motion.

The plastic baggy crinkles as I take it from my pocket, swiping her wine glass and raising it to inspect the contents. Half a glass. After a moment of consideration, I take a gulp, halving it.

That's probably not too much.

Opening the baggy, I quickly pour the powder inside, swirling it around with hard flicks of my wrist.

I reach below the table to give my dick an understanding squeeze as I push the glass back to her side of the table, but even though my blood is already rushing in anticipation, annoyance gnaws at my thoughts. This shit is just way too easy.

Oops, I spilled something on you?

She bought that?

I'm going to have to sit my little sister down after this and have a serious discussion about vigilance.

It eases a bit when she returns. I might have done my recon, but we're still in North Side. Letting her out of my sight long enough to drug her drink was always going to be the hardest part about this.

I mean.

Aside from my dick.

Her dress flutters out around her thighs as she takes her seat, scooting close. "I'm sure I can get the stain out with the right soak. No harm done."

Gruffly, I say, "good," and watch with thinly veiled fascination as she grabs her glass, lifting it to her pink lips. Her throat jumps with a petite swallow, but when she sets the glass back down, her face puckers strangely.

She peers into the wine glass. "This tastes…" There's another grimace, but it falls away when her gaze meets mine, eyes widening. "Oh."

Feeling cagey, I look away. "You said I could pick the time."

She glances back at the wine, a pensive expression crossing her face. "Huh. Tonight?"

Somewhere in the back, dishes clatter, but my gaze is narrowed in on hers as I reach beneath the table, grazing my fingertips against her bare inner thigh. "Tonight."

Her mouth parts, a dazed look coming over her eyes. "Right. Of course. You said… you said you wanted me all to yourself tonight." I can see the cogs working in her head, understanding what I meant by that. I want her *wholly* to myself.

I raise my chin, fixing her with a hard look. "Okay?" It comes out more challenging than I mean it to, but she understands, giving me her answer.

Never breaking my stare, she lifts the glass.

And downs it in three big gulps.

"Hey," her small hand squeezes my thigh. "I don't know if I can make it home."

I glance over and gently grab her chin, turning her face to me. Her eyes are soft. Glazed. I frown. "Already? It should take at least another ten minutes to kick in."

Adrenaline is already pumping in my veins—anticipation— but now it ratchets up a notch. When I'd asked her a few weeks ago, she'd been ridiculously willing to go along with it right then, but that's not how I wanted it. I wanted it like this.

Planned.

Detailed.

Ruthless.

"I know. I guess I'm a lightweight." The last word slurs at the end and her head droops to the side, before she jerks back up. "God. Is the truck spinning?"

Fucking Rath. Did he get the dosage off? No. No. It was probably too much wine to pair with it. Shit. My mind runs through the options. There aren't many. I could speed home, carry her upstairs and toss her in bed. Take her over to the park two blocks over, find a secluded spot and do this in the car? Fuck that. Not enough space or time, and getting busted by the park cops isn't one of my fantasies.

The light turns red and I stop, tucking my arm around her

shoulders. "Hold on, baby. I'll figure this out."

That's when I take in my surroundings. *Where* we are. It's the ambiguously neutral part of North Side people don't talk about. It's so familiar that it faded into the background when I passed it on the way to the restaurant. I press the gas before the light fully changes, taking a hard left into the entrance of a neighborhood. No, not just a neighborhood. My neighborhood, where I grew up. The house where I met her.

My father left it to me when he died, and I've had zero desire to set foot in it again.

But desperate times…

Giving her a small shake, I insist, "Talk to me, Story. Stay awake. Just a few more minutes."

She gives a long, happy sigh, and I can't help but watch her cleavage swell with it. "Your truck is comfy," she says, head lolling.

"Shit." I spot the house ahead. Compared to the other well-lit houses surrounding it, the place practically looks abandoned.

It basically is.

She blinks as I pull into the driveway, squinting forward. "Are we at…?"

Cutting the ignition, I answer, "Home sweet home, little sister. You think you can walk to the door?"

"Sure," she says but it comes out slurred and airy. "I just want to sleep for you, babe."

Sleep. She means letting me drug and fuck her. Just hearing her say it makes my dick swell. "God, I love you, you know that?"

She nods, eyes drooping. I lean over and kiss her anyway, tasting the sweet chocolate from her dessert, the warm, barely-responsive heat of her tongue. Making sure she's stable against the seat, I exit the truck and walk around to her door, pulling it open. It's pretty obvious there's no way she's walking in the house on her own. I glance around, making sure no nosy neighbors are out, and lean in to scoop her up into my arms. I ease her out, shut the truck door with my foot and carry her around to the entrance, fighting the sensation of déjà vu. There, I use the keycode to open it, not breathing until we're safe inside.

"You still with me?" My voice slices through the eerie silence of the house just as I flick on a light.

"Uh huh."

Her head slumps against my arm and I tighten my grip on her, keeping her neck braced. It's hard to move forward. She's so fucking beautiful like this, flushed from the wine, drifting slowly into unconsciousness, my cock growing harder with every passing minute.

My eyes dart around the room. Everything is exactly the way Posey left it. The brocade chair I've dreamt of bending Story over a million times, the formal dining room table where I could spread her out and feast on her all night. The kitchen counter, the lambskin ottoman, the antique sideboard... and Jesus Christ, the top of the washing machine in the laundry room.

"Every goddamn room," I mutter to myself. I've got a whole list of places in this house I wish I'd fucked her, and so far, I've only managed to nail her on my father's desk. Shit, if I don't get inside her soon, I'm going to come in my pants like a fourteen-year-old getting his first taste of porn.

But even as I catalogue the places I want to take—*defile*—my girl, there's only one place I've ever really dreamed of fucking her while she's asleep in this house: My bed.

I've had the fantasy a million times. In it, I'd come home from practice, sweaty from a long, hard workout. Her door would be closed, her soft voice or music barely audible. I'd shower and jerk off, knowing I couldn't have her, releasing my frustration onto the wet, slippery tiles. Nowhere close to being satisfied, I'd jump out and towel off, but when I'd return to my room, I'd find her there. Asleep in *my* bed.

A lamb for the slaughter.

The reality is so much better, though.

I carry her up the stairs and down the hall, past her old room, and right into mine. There's a moment where I'm clutching her close, frozen in the doorway as I survey the space. It's like walking into a time capsule. My posters are still on the wall. My jerseys. My trophies. There's even a stick of deodorant sitting on my dresser, almost as if I'd woken up one day, bolted in the middle of getting ready for the drive to high school, and never returned.

I guess that was pretty much what happened.

I don't fight the strange dissonance of it. Tonight was never about moving forward. It's about going back. The more I think about it, the more fitting it feels to do this here, in the same bed I used to stroke myself in while thinking about her, just a single wall away.

Carefully, I lay her on the bed. She lets out a little sigh, eyes fluttering, and squeezes my fingers before her head drops to the side.

I know she's out when the confused crease in her forehead disappears entirely.

For a moment, I just stand back and stare, the bottom of her dress all rucked and twisted, revealing a milky swath of her perfect inner thigh. Her hair is fanned out on the pillow—*my* pillow—and her flushed chest rises and falls with slow, even breaths.

God, she's gorgeous.

I wouldn't have known it back then, but it's better this way. Fucking her here, like this, might be my teenage wet dream, but as I shuck off my jacket, I try to remember that it's something bigger than that.

It's a gift.

Story's giving this to me because that's how much she loves

me—*trusts* me. She believes in me so much that she's fine with being unconscious like this, willingly giving over her body to me.

The first thing I do is turn down the lights, nothing but the lamp on the bedside table illuminating the room. It makes her look somehow softer, quieter. The second thing I do is press a fingertip to her throat, feeling her pulse thrum as I glide it down her sternum, over the initial I carved there.

Pressing a knee into the mattress, I trail my finger to the right, raising another to pluck at the other side of her dress's neckline. All that covers her breasts are two tall triangles, and I hook my fingers into each.

Slowly, I part the fabric.

Her tits spill out, so round and perfect that I can't stand to see them as they are, nipples hiding away beneath the flesh.

Bending down, I extend my tongue to lick one into a hard peak. It never takes much with her, but I take my time anyway, releasing a gruff sound when her breath hitches.

"Shh." I move to the other nipple, already hardening, and suck it to a point. My lips move against it. "You're mine now, little sister–all of you."

When I glance up, she's perfectly still.

I lower my hand to her thigh, that enticing space where the dress ends and she begins, grazing the skin. She twitches, ticklish, but doesn't stir as I glide my fingers up, pushing the dress toward her waist.

"Fuck," I breathe as the juncture of her legs is revealed. I catch a glimpse of simple, thin, white cotton panties and have to reach down to give my dick a hard squeeze. "You know what you're doing, don't you?" I raise my gaze to her face, bending to lick a slow, wet kiss to her frozen lips.

I take my time stripping her down, threading her arms through the dress's straps, yanking it out from beneath her and over her hips. I don't know how she does it, finding the pieces that work for each of us. That's just how well she knows who we are, what we want. It's why there's no one but her.

When she's down to just her panties, I stand, removing my pants and shirt. My cock is painfully hard and I circle the bed until my hips are level with the edge. Turning her face toward me, I pump my dick hard, pushing the sticky clear fluid to the tip. Exhaling, I lean forward and press it to the plush give of her parted mouth, spreading it across her pink lips. It starts like this—always like this—and never fails to get the blood pumping in my veins.

"Open up, sweet girl," I say, thumbing her mouth open. Unlike the other times I've done this, there's no fear of waking her up. Not with the drugs running through her. And *Jesus*, it's even better than I thought it'd be, the certainty that I can do anything–fucking *anything*–to her, and it'll only be for me.

Her mouth parts and I push my way in, letting her hot tongue and cheeks surround me with warmth.

Carefully cradling the back of her head, I fuck her mouth nice and slow, taking care not to go too deep, too rough. Sometimes I get the feeling Rath and Tris… they think I like fucking Story when she's asleep because it means I can be as rough and nasty and savage as I want to be.

They're wrong.

Fucking her hard and angry is easy. Story would take it. Every inch. Every bruise. Every shove. She'd take it and she'd give it right back, because sometimes we're the hottest when it's a fight. Push and pull. Screams and grunts. There's nothing difficult about that.

It's so much harder to make love to her.

To caress her cheeks–caving on an instinctual suck–with a reverence verging on religious. To pull my dick out of her mouth and crouch down, thumbing the slickness from her lips as I whisper, "So good for me, little sister." To see her innocence and purity, and selfishly, *hungrily*, want it for myself.

When I finally crawl into bed beside her, my dick is dripping with eager precum, twitching impatiently. I gather it up with a shaky forefinger, only to immediately feed it to her through slack lips. I shudder at the look of it, the shine of her lips, sticky with me.

She's limp like a rag-doll, pliable and loose as I spoon up behind her, dragging her tightly into the curve of my body. I revel in the feeling for a moment, drawing it out, savoring what's to come. Story's so small. She fit at that tiny table in the restaurant, all delicate and sweet. But she fits just as well against my body and all of its hard angles and dark ink.

She's quiet and still as I palm the cut of her shoulder, trailing down her arm, brushing the side of her full tit, touching the tattoo on her wrist, sliding to the curve of her hips.

She's already getting slick when I push my fingers between her legs.

I bury a groan into her neck as I rub lazy circles into her clit, rocking my dick into the warm cleft of her ass. It takes everything in me not to plow inside and *take*–to get her loose and ready for me. But I'm not here to tear her up.

"The first time I thought about taking you like this, sweet girl," as I reach behind me for the bedside table drawer, "was when my dad taunted and teased you with me. But now you're mine." Under the skin magazines and boxes of out-of-date condoms is a bottle of lube.

I pour a pool into the palm of my hand and with the other, push down her panties and spread her, running my fingers between her cheeks.

It's not the first time I've fingered her ass, and I know just how she likes it. I massage the tight ring of muscle first, feeding it my fingertip slowly. My eyes rove her naked, slack body as I push in to the first knuckle, jaw clenched at the sensation. She's hotter here than anywhere, her asshole fluttering weakly around me.

The second finger makes that crease in her forehead reappear, and I soothe it away with a kiss to her temple, whispering, "You can take it, little sister. Your body's meant for me. You feel that, don't you? The way you open up for me so willingly? It's because you're not whole without a part of me inside you."

Against the pillow, her fingers twitch.

"That's right," I whisper, glad she's not awake to hear my voice rasp when I grab my dick, sliding the head through the slick crevice of her ass. "I'm going to give you what you want."

The sound I make when I finally push inside is barely human. I dig my fingers into her hip as I force my way through the tight, puckered ridge of her ass.

The only sound in the house is my hissed, "Goddamn it." I press my forehead to her shoulder and breathe.

This isn't going to last nearly as long as I want it to.

Dragging in a ragged inhale, I push her to her stomach, rolling over her back. The effort it takes to pose her, lifting her hips so I can tuck her knees beneath her, is enough to distract me from coming for a while. But once she's face-down, ass in the air, it all gets so much worse.

I can see with crystal-clear, HD clarity, what her ass looks like swallowing my cock. "Christ, look at you." My eyes never leave the sight as I pull back, watching her puckered hole twitch with every drag of my cock. Burying it back inside is even better, my hips pushing into her limp, silent body. Reaching up, I sweep her hair away from her cheek, curling over her to push a kiss into it. "Can't wait to come for you, little sister."

I fuck into her deep and slow, hips curling and snapping. I alternate between watching her ass take me in, and watching different parts of her body be jostled by the force of it. With every thrust, my balls draw tighter and tighter, my strokes growing shorter and more purposeful. I wish I could make it last, have her like this every night.

But I can't stop the inevitable.

I'm panting into her cheek, hand fisted tightly into the crown of her hair, when I lurch to a shuddering halt, releasing a mangled groan. My whole body jerks with the force of it, cock pumping hot and slick surges of cum deep into her ass.

I finish with a slam of my hips as the fist tangled in her hair pushes her down into it, keeping it all inside, as deep as it can go.

And then the tension snaps, leaving me breathless and lazy.

Easing her back to her side, I embrace her, chest heaving from exertion. She's got to still be unconscious, but I freeze when her hips rock, pushing her ass back into me. Levering up onto my elbow, I rise up and watch her, tucking a lock of her hair away.

Her eyes are closed, lashes soft against her cheeks, breathing even, but her hips give the slightest thrust, and there's a tightness to her mouth that wasn't there before.

I smirk, whispering, "Still horny, aren't you?" into the shell of her ear. "Want me to get you off?"

I skim her arms, her belly, her tits, with my fingertips. Her nipples are already hard peaks, her skin covered in gooseflesh. Pulling out, I spread her legs and scoop the cum oozing from her hole just a scant couple inches northward, spreading it messily into her wet folds. She might not be conscious, but her body still responds, hips rolling against the heel of my palm.

A soft breath of a moan spills from her throat.

"I've got you," I answer, brushing over her clit. I kiss her neck, her shoulders, the swell of her breasts. I push my cum inside her pussy, fucking her with my fingers, and it's not long before her breath changes, turning into short pants.

"Come on, baby," I say to her. "Come for your big brother."

Suddenly, her hand slides over mine, the first real movement she's made since I brought her upstairs. "Killian," she breathes, hips rising, pussy tightening. "Oh, god."

Her eyes never open, but her pussy clenches, wrapping around my fingers as the orgasm shudders through her. I let her ride it out, taking cues from her body, until she melts back into the bed, once again settling into a deep sleep. I curl into her, feeling my cock getting hard again, but allow my own exhaustion to take over.

THERE'S NO FOOD in the house, so I have it delivered. Specifically, the greasy stuff from down at the diner—cheesy eggs and hash browns, crispy bacon. The shit Tris never lets her have. I rummage through the pantry once it's arrived, searching for something to plate it with. The house was left almost exactly the way it was when Posey was hauled off by the police, but a cleaning lady did empty the refrigerator. This apparently included a complete de-kitchening.

Stumped, I glare into the empty cabinets. "Where the fuck are the plates?"

I could just take it up in the takeout containers it came in, but after what I did to her last night? She deserves more than a styrofoam box.

It hits me–the garage. Posey always used to store all the fancy guest plates in the cabinets there. I take one step in and flinch, face scrunching. "Jesus Christ!"

God, the smell. Flipping on the light, I cover my mouth and nose, trying to figure out what the fuck I'm looking at. What the hell the smell is.

A huge metal dog crate sits in the middle of the room, wires leading up to it from the breaker panel. There's also a bucket in the corner. Brown paper fast food bags are wadded up on the floor. I get as close as I can, and yep. That smell?

It belongs to whatever's in the bucket.

I toe the bags over, revealing a smiling taco logo.

Someone's been in here–in *there*–inside that dog crate, and it sure as hell wasn't a dog. I spend a moment trying to fit the pieces together, but quickly wash my hands of it. Whatever the hell happened down here, I decide I'm better off not knowing. Not today. If I tracked down every deviant thing my father did, I'd never have time for anything else.

Deciding styrofoam will just have to fucking do, I shut the door, bolt it, and go back inside.

She's still asleep when I get back upstairs, curled into my empty spot. I rest the tray of food on the bedside table and go into the bathroom, running a washcloth under the faucet. With the warm cloth in my hand, I return, sitting on the edge of the bed and pushing her hair off her face. She shifts, squirming under the blanket, and burrows down deeper into the pillow. Stifling a laugh, I bend and kiss her forehead. I'm really better at keeping her asleep than waking her up.

She sniffs, nose wrinkling, and then opens her eyes.

"Hey," she says in a sleep-thick voice, eyes blinking into focus.

"Good morning." I gently tug at the blanket, revealing her tits. I hold up the washcloth. "I thought you may need to clean up a little."

She cranes her neck, looking down, and rubs at a patch of

dried cum. I watch carefully as she takes it in, a twinge of worry forming in the pit of my gut. It was easy for her to agree to this a couple weeks ago, but now that it's done, maybe she'll have regrets.

Her eyes find mine, a wry grin tugging at her mouth as she stretches. "Guess it wasn't just my pussy you fucked last night."

I track the pull and shift of her muscles, the way her tits lengthen with the bow of her back. "Do you want to know?" I ask.

Mouth, ass, pussy, tits... pussy again. She was out for hours, and I made the best use of the time.

She hums, kicking the blanket off. "Only if I had a good time?"

This is easy to answer. "Oh yeah, I made sure of it." She's soft and lazy as I help her get cleaned up, running the cloth between her breasts and legs. I did what I could the night before, but... she looked too damn good covered in my cum to do much about it. When I toss her an old t-shirt from my dresser, she pulls it on and digs into breakfast.

She takes a bite of bacon and groans, and the flutter inside isn't just down at my cock. It's in my chest. God, this girl—this woman—I love her so much.

"Hey," I say, grabbing her attention. "Thank you for letting me do that." I squeeze her thigh, because I'm not stupid. I know I'm sort of a creep, liking what I like–actually fucking needing it sometimes. It's one thing for her to indulge me with it sometimes. It's another for her to embrace it.

Giving me a strange look, she says, "I'm your Lady," and leans forward to press her greasy lips against mine. "I trust you with my life."

I sit next to her, grabbing my own container, and lean back on the headboard. Her hair is adorably messy, my oversized shirt unintentionally sexy. Watching her, a warmth spreads through my chest. Not horniness. Something else.

Whatever expression I'm making, she catches it, asking over a mouthful of eggs, "What?"

"Nothing." I shrug. "I like this."

"Eggs?"

"Breakfast in bed with you," I clarify. "More than fancy French food. Or lacy dresses. Or even what we did last night."

All those years of wanting her in my bed–*this bed*–I didn't know that just having her here with me like this, would mean just as much. Last night, I had this passing thought that I wanted her like that every night. Unconscious. Easily used. Posed however I wanted her. It was hot as fuck, I won't deny that.

But I need her like this even more.

It's a huge fucking revelation.

"I like it, too." She eyes the side of pancakes I ordered for myself. "Can I have some of that?"

Snorting, I push it over, trying to shake off the epiphany. She cuts off a huge piece and crams it into her mouth, so ravenous that it's almost impressive.

"Hey, you'll never believe the weird shit I just saw in the garage."

"Oh yeah?" she asks, voice muffled around a bite of pancake.

"A dog crate," I say, scratching my head. "And there was a bucket in the corner. I'll spare you the details of what I found inside of it, but someone had obviously been held captive in there."

The fork stops halfway to her mouth, eyes unblinking. "Oh. That *is* crazy. Do you know who did it?"

Head shaking, I answer, "No, and honestly, I don't want to."

"Good idea," she replies, shoving the pancake in her mouth. "Best to let sleeping dogs lie. But then, you're good at that, aren't you?" The borderline sleazy wink she gives me sends all my blood south.

"Well, I don't see any dogs here…," Reaching out, I sling my arm around her shoulders, tugging her up against me.

We're both leaning back and her eyes skim the room. "Fuck it's weird being in here."

"Yeah?"

"God yes, I was terrified to even walk past your door." She looks up at me. "You were so quiet in here. Angry. I felt like you were always just… plotting something."

I laugh, because, Jesus, she has no idea. "I had a lot of shit going on back then. It's probably better if you don't know." I squeeze her against my side. "But I'm glad you're awake again."

"Me too." She sets down her plate and rises to her knees, slinging her leg over my hips. Straddled, she links her arms around my neck and kisses me, syrupy sweet. "Because there are a lot of things we can also do while I'm awake, and I really don't want to miss out on them."

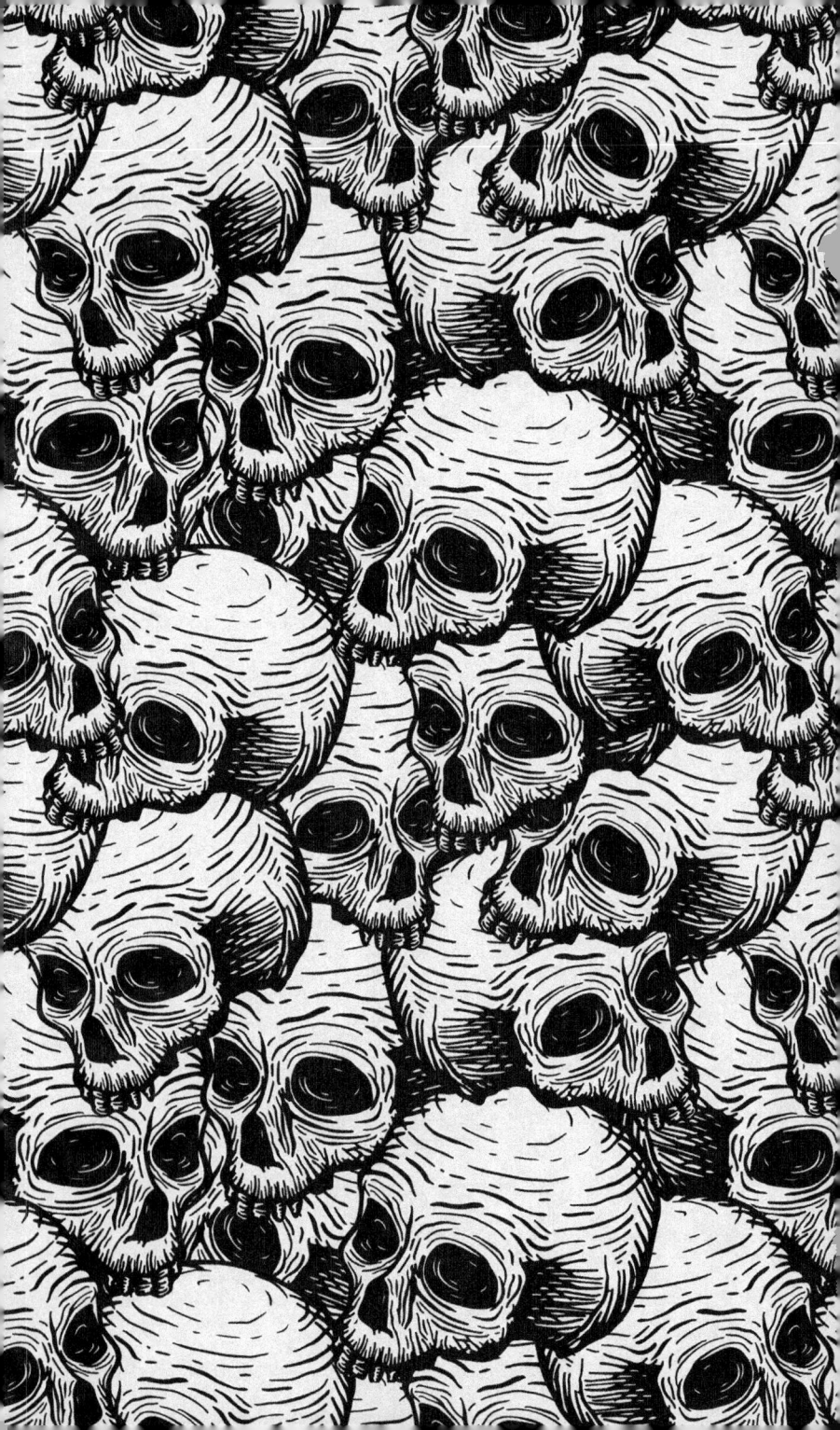

DIMITRI
RATHBONE

APRIL

GLARING, I ASK, "Remind me why I agreed to this again?"

I'm standing outside a room full of small, obnoxious demons. I can see them through the window, running wild, their voices loud and shrill, and still barely audible over the disharmonious shrieks of the recorders they're all holding.

I bet they smell bad, too. Kids always do.

Fuck every square inch of my dick.

"It's your turn to spend a day with the kids," Story says. "Killian already had three football scrimmages with them, and Tristian comes weekly to tutor them with the laptops his dad donated." She pokes me in the side. "You're up."

"These kids don't give a shit about classical music." I go to cross my arms, but think better of it. I'll never live it down if I sulk. "And even if they did, having it played on those devil sticks might actually be a crime against humanity."

Story rolls her eyes. "Then teach them something else.

You're not all Chopin and Beethoven, or whatever." Her eyes brighten as she holds out a blue, plastic recorder. "What about *Twinkle, Twinkle, Little–*"

I give the recorder the most hostile stare imaginable. "No!"

"Listen here, you little rat-faced twatwaffle," Mrs. Crane says, thrusting a finger at me. "You go in there and teach them to play something on this goddamn recorder, or I'll shove it so far up your ass, your sneezes will sound like a fucking symphony."

I narrow my eyes at the old woman. "Why are you here again?"

"Because your Lady's my ride." She jerks her thumb at Story. "And apparently you needed someone to kick your ass."

Story has been running 'errands' with Delores for a while now. No one knows what they're about, but Killian figures someone should keep an eye on her until we figure it out.

"Dimitri," Story says, gripping my leather jacket. I know she's pulling out the big guns when she gives me that *look*, all big-eyed and pleading. "Music means a lot to you. It gave you something amazing and safe. What if even one of those kids in there could find the same thing? What if they saw you–how good you are at it–and how it shaped your life? Got you into college. Gave you a purpose." She pats my chest, imploring. "You can show them–tell them about how you got here."

I gaze into her eyes. "You want me to tell them that I was illiterate, passed from one grade to the next, charmed my way to graduation, and then convinced my house girl to give me blow jobs and teach me to read?"

"Dimitri!" Story hisses, jaw dropping as she swats my shoulder. "Oh my god."

I snatch the recorder from her, eyes narrowing. "Who the hell donated these, anyway? We could have gotten a piano, you know." I'm going to really miss the piano when we move out of the LDZ house. The long nights spent composing on it. The mornings eating my girl out on top of it. Leaving it behind is bad enough. "Hell, I would have settled for some string instruments. But this?" I wave the recorder in her face.

Plastic, bullshit, awful-sounding recorders?

This is a personal attack.

As her eyes shutter, I step closer. "*Tell me.*"

Cagily, she looks away. "It was anonymous."

"Bullshit," I say. "I want to know who had the fucking *gall* to—"

"I did." My head whips around to Mrs. Crane, who raises her chin in defiance. "I donated them, shithead. All seventy-five of them. Cheap as hell, too."

I gawk at her, staring her up and down. "You evil, scheming, spiteful bitch."

"Aw." She touches her chest. "You're not just saying that?"

It dawns on me. "This is payback because of last week, isn't it? I told you, I had to lay down that tuba track in the kitchen because of the acoustics. I didn't know you were taking a nap!"

"Your head really is full of nothing but rocks and spunk, isn't it?" Mrs. Crane sneers at me. "Your girl's got the plot, jizzstain. You've got something almost no one else in this town does: *Talent*. One of those little crotch goblins might have it, too. And you're gonna go show them what that looks like."

Groaning, I swing my gaze to Story. "I thought I was going to take you on a date."

And get laid.

"You will," she assures, ushering me toward the room. "After this."

"Fine." I run my hand through my hair. "But I won't be held responsible for any tears or future emotional damage."

"Thank you." Story rises up on her toes and kisses my cheek. "You'll do great."

I take a deep breath, similar to how I prepare myself to walk in the DKS ring at Friday Night Fury–or when I'm facing down the Baron King whenever we need some... work handled. It's not like they're a shadowy cabal of dead-body-disappearers.

They're just kids.

But I'm a Lord. My best friend is a King. I can play Bach's Chaconne in D minor without sheet music, for fuck's sake. Glancing at Story, I remember that I also get to fuck the prettiest goddamn woman in all of Forsyth. Maybe Mrs. Crane doesn't have it all wrong. I've got a lot to offer.

I open the door and stride through them, ears ringing from the chaos.

Clearing my throat, I call out, "Everyone settle down," and move to the front of the room. There are rows of seats, thankfully bolted to the floor. Unthankfully, no one is sitting in any of them. They're too busy running around the room, blowing hot air into their god-awful, sorry excuses for instruments. "Listen up!" I try again, bringing my palms together in a loud clap. "It's time to get started!"

The only response is a sea of wailing recorders.

Fuck. I knew this was a bad idea. I can't even get them to listen. I glance at Story, and she gestures eagerly for me to try again.

"Alright, that's enough! Everyone—" Suddenly, a wad of paper smacks me in the cheek. I catch the eye of the little punk that threw it at me and lunge forward.

A hand pushes me back, and an old, frail force of nature steps between me and the room.

"You little shitheads better give me five!" Mrs. Crane shouts. Her hand is in the air, fingers splayed and ticking down. "Five... four... three... two! That's right. I want to see all of your little shrieking butts in a seat." She swings her glare at the paper thrower. "Hey, you! Something wrong with your butt?"

He shakes his head and drops into the nearest chair.

She adjusts her purse on her shoulder, her narrowed gaze

passing over the audience. "This ninny-fuck over here is going to teach you how to breathe sounds that don't make me wish for the sweet oblivion of death. He might not be much to look at, but you're going to listen to what he says and do what he tells you to." A little girl in the front gulps as Mrs. Crane's glower lands on her. "Am I clear?"

A chorus of 'Yes ma'am's' fills the room.

"Good. You may learn something." She gives me a dubious look. "Or you may give this guy a splitting migraine in the middle of his day. Whatever happens, happens."

Bitch.

I knew this was payback.

She turns to leave but I rest a hand on her shoulder, hissing, "Wait! How the hell did you get them to listen to you?" A quick glance tells me these kids are ready to erupt the second she leaves the room.

Mrs. Crane scoffs, pulling a wrinkled pack of cigarettes from her purse. "Oh, they're easy. They haven't turned into hopeless shitbags yet. Can't say the same for the rest of you." At my baffled expression, she sighs, relenting, "Kids are like a Kingdom. You can't rule them on fear alone. They don't have to like you, but they damn sure have to respect you." She leaves me with a hard look. "That's just something you have to earn." Hitching her bag over her shoulder she adds, "I'll be in the car."

I know I need to get back to the kids before things get wild again, but I touch Story on the chin and say, "After all this—that date better be worth it."

THE HOUSE IS dark when I pull my Camaro up the secluded drive. With the landscaping having fallen to the wayside over the course of the sale, weeds are a little grown up around us. Tendrils of vines and forbidden dandelions swaying in a passing breeze are all that greets us. The windows stare down on us like empty eyes, as if it's been sitting here, hoping we'd arrive.

We've already toured it twice, and been by once to approve some roofing repairs, but this is the first time I feel truly stricken by this house.

It's been lonely.

Waiting.

When I look beside me, Story is gazing up at the empty-eye-windows, her mouth slack. It's probably the first time during the drive she's done something other than stroke the dash, gushing about the Chevy I've spent our senior year rebuilding over in Northridge. I've had it for three months, and even though it's not packing much beneath the hood, she still gets little stars in her eyes when she slips into my passenger seat. She and Tristian like their cars fast and full of muscle, but my old Chevy and I aren't built to race. We're made to swagger.

She loves it.

"I've never seen it at night," she breathes, ducking to peer up at the roofline. "Can you believe–"

"No." I cut the ignition, an odd feeling building in my gut. I've felt it a lot over the past few weeks. I'm on the deed–we all are. I've got a pair of keys, and I paid what I could, but it's still hard to think of this house as mine.

Ours.

The silence swells and when she finally tears her eyes away from the house, they level me with a dark, soft look.

"You've never had a home before," she guesses, her whisper cleaving through the stillness. "Not a real one."

Reaching out, I tuck a lock of hair behind her ear, indulging in the small shiver it elicits. "Neither have you." Probably the closest either of us have come is the brownstone. But that doesn't belong to us. It belongs to LDZ. We're comfortable there and it's familiar in a bone-deep way, but it can never be what we need.

Her mouth pulls into a soft grin. "Then we'll have to make this one ours."

I give the house another long, dubious look. "That's the idea."

The dinner I'd just treated her to sits heavy in my gut as I exit the car and round the front, wrenching open her door. My eyes slice nervously through the darkness, shoulders high and tight, as if I'm doing something criminal. I didn't ask the others before impulsively driving up here, and somehow it feels... wrong. Being here without them. As if I'm stealing something away by leading Story through its doors for the first time after the sale went through. They probably had big plans to mark the occasion. Killian and Tristian have been almost as excited as Story about getting this house.

But me?

Shit's weird.

Story noticed it over the dinner I took her to at our favorite Mexican joint. Tristian can keep taking her to East End health food places, and Killian can keep his French cuisine at North Side restaurants she can barely read the menus for. When my nights come to take our girl out, I give her the full South Side experience. It's not all whores and gutter muppets down here. We have Forsyth's best hole-in-the-walls.

Still a little tipsy from her margarita, she sways into me when she steps out of the car, chest bouncing with a quiet laugh as I steady her.

I smirk. "Anyone ever tell you you're a cheap date?"

She places her hand on my chest and grins up at me, winking. "Only for you, Dimitri."

It's been nineteen months since Story became my lady–over four years since I had my first taste of her–but the way she says my name still makes warmth swell inside my chest.

And the sway of her hips as she leads me up the path to

the house, her hand grasping mine, still makes my dick rock-fucking-hard.

The door is just as big and heavy as the brownstone's, but this one hasn't been fitted with Tristian's paranoid security system yet, which means all I need to do is slide the key in the lock, and then the deadbolt, and turn it.

The second I push it open, I'm reaching for the gun in my waistband, spine going rigid in alarm. Thrusting a hand out behind me, I tell Story, "Baby, stay back."

"What?" she's saying, but my eyes are scanning the tall foyer for figures. Movement.

There's an unmistakable glow coming from the room to our right. "Someone's here," I whisper, sliding her a dark, forceful look as I chamber a round in my pistol. "Go back to the car."

In the soft, flickering glow of the house, I can finally see the sweet flush of her cheeks, a breath of rueful laughter escaping her throat. "Jesus. I'm just never going to be able to surprise any of you, am I?" Gently, she places her hand on mine–the one fisting the pistol–and pushes it down. "There are candles, Dimitri. My doing. Stand down."

Even as her words penetrate, half of me is still on alert, gaze jumping to the dark corners. "Candles?"

Rolling her eyes, she pushes past me, unconcerned by the gruff, unhappy sound I make. "Like I said, it was supposed to be a surprise. Indulge me, would you?"

I don't put my gun away. Not immediately. The truth is, this place is new and strange. I don't know all the hiding spots. Those places that creak. The sounds that alert you to an intruder. The ways the house lets you know it's on your side.

Maybe this one isn't on ours.

As if hearing every last word of my own goddamn thoughts, Story turns to me with a concerned frown. "This is supposed to be our home." Reaching for my hand, she tilts her head, pinning me with a soft look. "Remember?"

Exhaling, I disarm the chamber of the pistol, tucking the gun away. "You came here?" I wonder. "Before...?" *Before the date?* No, that's not right. She was chaperoning Mrs. Crane around town before that.

"Killian and Tris," she explains, tugging me into the foyer. "They set it up for me. For the surprise."

"Surprise," I mutter, struggling to shake off the prickle of adrenaline left behind. It's like having violence blue balls. Skeptical, I wonder, "The candles are the surprise?"

Her shoes click on the hardwood floor as she leads me through the archway. "The candles are for light, Dimitri. The power hasn't been turned on yet." Once through the door, she turns to me, mouth slanted into a smirk as she gestures behind her. "*This* is the surprise."

The candles are still the first thing I see. So many of them, scattered everywhere, cast a living, flickering glow around the room. It's almost too bright, my eyes fighting to adjust after the darkness of night.

But then I see a void in the brightness. A pool of sleek shadow reflects the candlelight like a mirror. When all I do is stare, her arm winds through mine, and I can't tear my eyes away long enough to meet her gaze, but I can feel it, careful and intent.

"I know why leaving the brownstone is so hard for you," she says, following my gaze. "Well, a part of it, at least."

It's a piano.

Not just any piano, either.

I blink. "Is that a…?"

I can hear the smile in her voice, even though it's wound around a rueful tone. "I wanted to get you the best, so I knew right off it was Steinway or nothing. We couldn't find you a concert grand, though."

As if it'd matter.

It's still fucking enormous—a ballroom grand from the looks of it. "How the hell did you get this?" I ask. The one in the brownstone is far more petite, and she's not wrong. I haven't been looking forward to leaving it. These past two years, it's become a part of my nights—our nights—having the keys at my fingertips whenever I pleased. Waking up at three in the morning to the smallest sound, too alert for my own good, has been soothed away by it, filling the halls with Brahms and Pachelbel, the Misfits and Weezer, and *fuck*.

My own music, too.

I've been composing like a goddamn lunatic since Christmas, just knowing the day would come when I'd have to leave it all behind.

And now there's *this.*

Her temple rests against my shoulder, voice turning wistful. "I took this from you once, Dimitri. And I'm not just talking about you spending all your savings to buy me in the pit, either. I wish I hadn't–"

"Don't." I stop her before she can say she's sorry. Killer, Tris, and I earned every bit of what she gave to us, and plenty more. That night of the concert, standing on the stage in front of hundreds of people, feeling like an insect, watching my hopes and dreams shatter around me…

Something died that night.

Something that had been slowly killing me my whole life.

"I need to," she responds, meeting my gaze. "I'm sorry."

Pulling her close, I frame her face in my hands, hardening my jaw. "I can play music anywhere, for anyone. You never took that from me, because it was never about that. It was about feeling bigger than I was. It was about finding a future where I knew I belonged." Sweeping my thumb over the flushed apple of her cheek, I say, "But, sometimes you have to lose everything to figure out what you really want, and baby, it's right here."

Her eyes collapse, a tear rolling down her cheek as she curls a palm around my neck. When I kiss her, it's gentle, even though that's not what I feel. Mostly, I want to slam her into the floor and make her mine, all over again.

But I don't want her to mistake it for anger.

She thumbs at my lip ring in the middle of our tongues meeting. She always loves doing that, touching my metal, warming it with her flesh, and I let her drag it out.

Until her lips move against mine. "Play for me?" She stands back, gesturing to the piano, and I can see her releasing all that old hurt, letting it burn away in the glare of the candlelight.

Even as she wipes away the dampness on her cheek, her smile is no less blinding.

Unthinkingly, I shuck off my leather jacket, fingers already buzzing in anticipation. "What do you want to hear?"

"One of yours," she says, bounding over to the bench. She's wearing a tight, low-cut sweater that makes her tits seem like living things. Her short black skirt grazes bare thighs as she perches on the bench, arrowing my eyes down to calf-length leather boots, and I wonder if she even realizes it.

Our Lady still dresses for us.

I take a long moment to appreciate the piano, taking a tour of its curves, sliding a fingertip over the glossy surface. Aside from the music department's concert piano, this will unquestionably be the best instrument I've ever played.

Story's gaze tracks me like an electric thrum, watching

me open the lid to ogle the pins and strings. The one in the brownstone is nice, but it needs some serious maintenance.

This one is fucking *pristine.*

I prop the lid for optimal sound, rucking up my sleeves to take my place on the bench.

Right beside her.

We do it back home–at the brownstone–like this sometimes, Story at my side as I get lost in the music. Sometimes late at night, I don't even realize it, startling out of some half-awake trance only to realize she's curled beside me, blinking sleepily as she smoothes my hair from my face.

My fingers hover over the keys for a moment as I try to choose a song, but I already know what she wants to hear. The second my fingers find the C-sharp, her mouth quirks into a quick grin.

"I love this one," she says.

"I know."

She doesn't speak at first. That's one of the things I love about her. Other people, other girls–hell, even Tristian and Killer–they think a song is a conversation, but Story knows better.

It's a breath.

Every crescendo is an inhale, every forte, an exhale.

The composition–a sonata with a bit of a 'fuck you' motif– begins with a slow, lonely tempo. It's her favorite of mine. I've played it for her so many times, I could probably nail it in my sleep. She lowers her head to my shoulder and listens to the breath of it, the bellow.

I'm halfway into the reprise when I feel her fingertip on my knee.

I lower my gaze unflinchingly, hands flying deftly over the keys as I watch her finger lazily ascend. It's only then that I realize she's been humming along under her breath. It's that, just as much as where her hand is going, that makes my dick grow stiff and painful.

Bench posture isn't really conducive to boners, and I shift, spreading my knees wider when her palm presses warmly to the bulge in my pants.

Without looking at her, my mouth tugs into a smirk. "So it's like that?"

She never stops humming, just casually begins unbuttoning my fly. We've all been so preoccupied with finals lately that it's been a while since I've felt her hand on my cock. That was the whole point of me taking her out tonight, so cum-brained that I'd probably do anything.

Like teaching fifteen kids how to play *Twinkle, Twinkle, Little Star* on recorders.

Adulthood and obligations and responsibility... it's all a fucking cockblock.

Now, the spark of warmth as she tugs me from my boxers makes my jaw clench tight. "Fuck," I mutter, struggling to keep my eyes open. I only allow my gaze to drop for a split-second, long enough to catch a glimpse of her palm closing around my shaft. "I know what you're doing," I say, voice a touch too gruff as I keep playing.

Her voice washes over my ear. "Playing my own instrument?"

My toes curl when her fingers squeeze the head. "Trying to trip me up. Won't work."

"I'd never try to trip you up," she responds, actually sounding genuine. "Actually, I want you to keep playing."

And then she's off the bench.

On her knees.

My eyes fly up to the keys. "Shit." I barely saw a flash of those dark eyes shining up at me from between my legs, but it's enough to make me shudder. "Baby, don't–" I swallow, trying to keep the tempo. "Don't tease. I've been hard for *days*."

Her palms skate up my thighs, warm and delicate. "Who's teasing?"

The hot shock of her tongue on my dick almost makes me lose it. *Almost.* I throw what little attention I can into playing as she swirls the slick tip of her tongue around my head. My teeth gnash together as I flex my hips upward, impatient and forceful.

Story takes it, though.

She opens her jaw wide for me, sucking me down with a low, musical hum. The groan that punches from my chest is a weak, pitiful thing, nothing like the harmony of her own moan as she glides her mouth up my shaft.

I'd know that sound anywhere.

"Show me," I demand, already halfway to panting like a dog for it. "I want to taste how wet you are for me."

Just as deftly as my hands move over the keys, her mouth works me, hand rising from between her legs. I can't see it, but I can hear in the sounds she makes that she's been touching herself.

Generously, she offers up her two slick fingers.

They slide between my lips just as her mouth goes down, throat tight against the tip of my cock. It's too much–the humming, the taste of her, the slick heat of her tongue–but the music is muscle memory, notes swelling around us as I taste her, and it makes it sound that much sweeter.

The end of the decrescendo is a sonorous tempo. It's a part of the movement I can play one-handed–for a time.

I use it to grab her by the hair.

Tangling it into a tight fist, I fuck up frantically into her mouth, and from the gentle sound she makes, she's expecting it, knowing all too well the peaks and valleys of the piece.

The heavy, dazed look she peers up at me with almost makes me bust.

"No," she gasps, my dick sliding from between her lips. "Don't come yet." Then, she reaches down, shifting and shimmying. I don't realize why at first, too busy being put-out by the lack of mouth on my cock. I really need both hands for the next part of the piece, so all I can do is watch dumbly as she contorts and grunts, ultimately lifting a scrap of black, lacy fabric.

Her panties.

With a breathless smile, she tucks them into my pants pocket, saying, "You might need those later. But not tonight." I spit a low, gritty curse as she rises, lifting a knee onto the bench beside me, then the other, straddling me.

The kiss is one of those wild, nasty situations where it's half teeth and half desperation. If my hands weren't currently occupied with pressing the keys, I'd be holding her face in a hard, bruising grip. But all I can do is grunt as Story reaches between us, grasping my cock and guiding it to her entrance.

She only pauses for a moment before sinking down.

For the first time, my fingers miss a note. "Fuck," I pant against her lips, struggling to find the tempo. "*Fuck*, you're soaked."

"Keep going," she whispers in a ragged voice. "The song isn't over yet."

Frustrated, I growl, "No one's that good at playing piano."

Who the fuck am I? God?

She exhales, long and slow, and I can see in the flicker of candlelight that her eyes are clenched tight as she settles, adjusting. "You feel so…" Her eyes flutter open, pinning me with an intensity that's almost too much. "Keep going," she urges.

I obey, fingertips mapping out the ivory.

Cum-brained motherfucker.

The first rock of her hips pulls a grunt out of me, thighs flexing. The second rock of her hips draws a gasp from her lips, and I swallow it greedily, blindly mashing the keys. I could be playing the sonata or *Twinkle, Twinkle, Little Bullshit Star* for all the care I put into the performance. Every cell of my being is narrowed down to the way she's riding me, my dick buried deep inside her. With every roll of her hips, arms wound tight around my neck, my balls get a little tighter. Eventually, I realize she's riding me to the tempo of the music, and–I mean...

The coda can be hard and fast.

Every composer makes edits and improvisations.

I kick the rhythm up a notch, just enough to feel her responsiveness, but not enough to be dissonant. She throws her head back, the column of her neck all slender and inviting, and I latch onto it, sucking a hard mark just below her jaw.

"Ah!" she gasps, grinding down into me as the tempo rises. It's not the first time I've played two instruments at once, but it's without a fucking doubt the most satisfying.

"Have you missed my dick, baby?" I tuck my nose into that spot beneath her ear–the one that always makes her shudder–before making my fingers move faster. "That's why you stopped before, isn't it? You want me to fill you up."

"Yes," she answers, always so unfiltered when she's like this, rosy-cheeked and out of breath. "I wanted–I want to feel you inside when you... *god...*"

My fingers move faster, jaw clenched as I feel her crashing into me with roll after roll of her hips, her movements growing precisely as frantic as the music. I know this pussy like the back of my hand. I don't even need to feel it to know how swollen and ripe her clit is right now. The way she's chasing it. The sweat dampening her skin. The soft, agonized sounds she's making...

It wouldn't take hardly anything at all.

The crescendo builds to a brutal tempo that has the tendons in my forearms straining with the ache of it, and for each press of the keys, she keens and fucks me just a little harder. My whole body is strung as tight as the wires inside the piano when she finally comes, clenching hard around me with the final savage note I slam into the keys.

I've got her bare ass banging a disharmonic *plunk* onto them so fast that she's still fluttering around me when my fingers finally dig into the soft flesh of her hips. The bench behind me makes a screeching noise as I spring up, slamming into her with an animalistic sound. Her nails dig painfully into the nape of my neck, clawing me closer, but it's unnecessary. I'm already curling over her as I fuck into the cradle of her thighs, the rhythm just as fast and fierce as the coda was.

She's just straining up to kiss me when I come, fireworks exploding behind my eyelids. My final thrusts are followed by the abrupt crash of keys, until the last of my cum is inside of her, buried deep.

She laughs, tongue still in my mouth and I pull back, too fuck-fogged to be offended. "What's so funny?" I pant.

"I'm just thinking about how that sounded, so beautiful and precise when you were playing on your own. And then I got involved, and it's nothing but chaos."

I pull back to give her a puzzled look. "The fuck are you talking about? *That* was a masterpiece." My head tilts, considering it. "I think I'll call it… 'Homecoming'. Although it definitely needs some fine-tuning."

Her lips curve upward. "Practice you mean?"

"Repeated."

Her head tilts back in a laugh. "God, the neighbors are going to hate us."

I don't give a shit about neighbors, or the fact I just desecrated tens-of-thousands-of-dollars worth of piano by letting Story's wet pussy drip onto the keys. I just care about the fact that for the first time, no one can take this away from me.

Home.

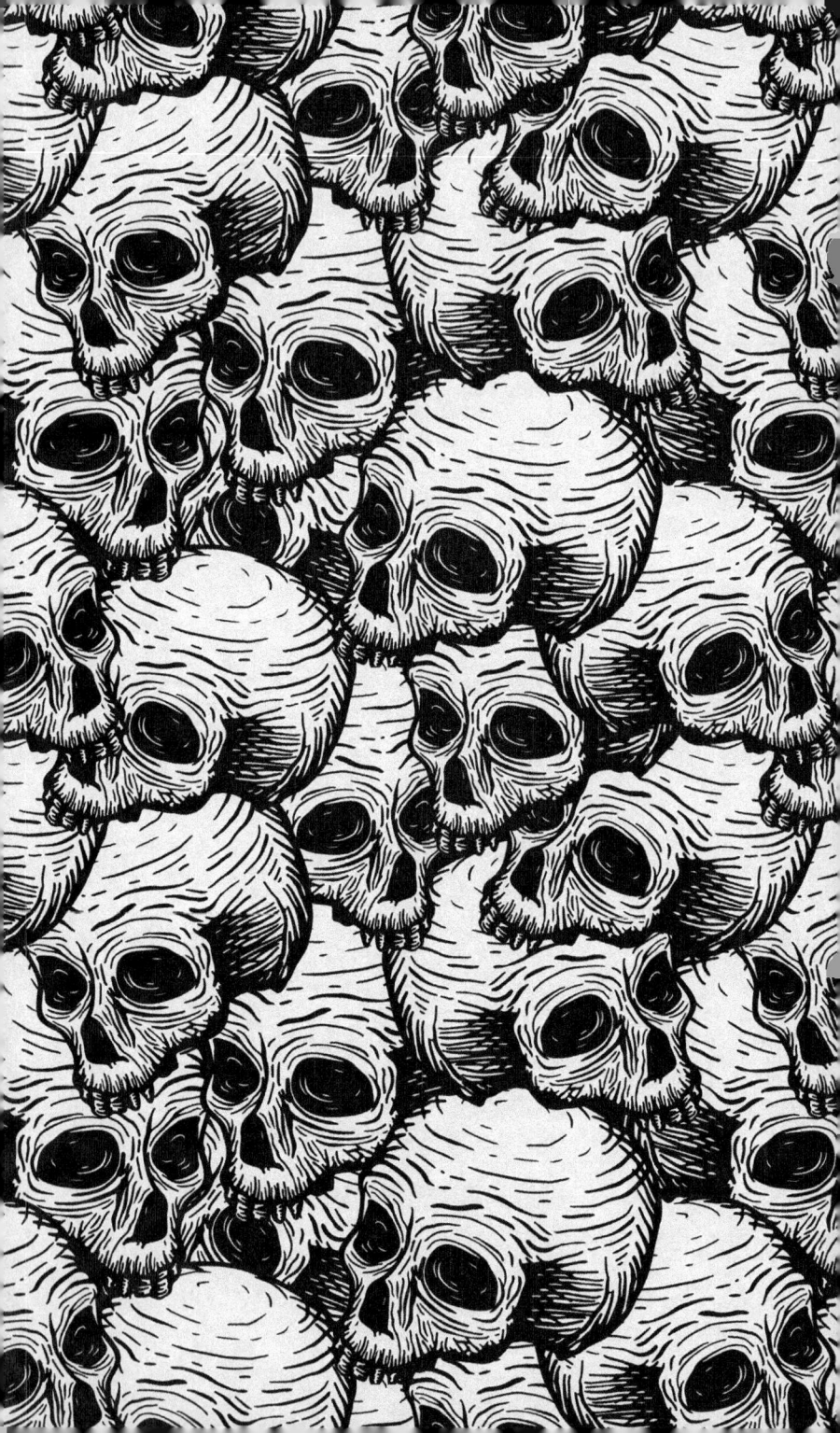

TRISTIAN
MERCER

JULY

"We have people to do that," I say, watching Story climb off the boat and down to the dock.

She rolls her eyes. "I don't need a servant to go into the convenience store for me, Tris."

I scramble. "Fuck, then hold on–let me get my shoes." I shove them on and grab the little white dress off the lounge chair, following her off the boat.

There are a lot of perks about coming from a wealthy family. Access. Privilege. Gluttony. All come into play on days like today: clear blue skies, fresh clean water, drinks, a little weed, a magnificent sunset, and my sexy girl in nothing but the skimpy two-piece I bought for her just for the holiday.

Which is also the reason I've been not-so-discreetly sporting a semi all day.

Traditionally, the Counts are all about the Fourth of July. They have a massive barbeque with tons of food, music, and impressive fireworks. Unfortunately, after Lavinia Lucia blew up her family home, *with* her father still inside, that event is no longer taking place. It did open the door for my father to approach the town council and volunteer to fund the fireworks display.

My itch for pyrotechnics may be genetic.

I catch up to Story halfway down the dock, flustered and sweating. "Jesus, you know you can't just walk around here like it's the goddamn Avenue."

"What are you talking about?"

I wave a hand, incredulous. "This is Count territory." True, the Counts have been blown–both figuratively and literally–to smithereens. But territory lines aren't so easily erased. I pat the gun in the back of my trunks. "You can't walk around here unguarded." I look down at the fabric in my hand, thrusting it toward her. "Oh, and put this on."

She blinks down at the cover-up. "We're at a marina, Tris. On the Fourth of July. It's hot, I'm covered in sunscreen, and no one cares that I'm walking around in my bathing suit."

To prove her point, a group of swimsuit-clad girls pass us, climbing onto a speedboat tied to a nearby slip. Proving *my* point, a group of four teenage boys hanging around the fishing area turn to ogle her.

Story keeps walking and I follow, grabbing her arm to pull her to a stop. "Sweetheart, as much as I get the appeal of you flaunting your gorgeous body and making everyone jealous that they're not me, I can't let you do it."

She looks fucking obscene, her bottoms tied on her hips, her top one string-tug away from popping off altogether. It wouldn't matter in South Side. There, everyone knows who she is, who she belongs to. LDZ would avert their goddamn eyes, because they respect us.

Here, no one does.

"Seriously?" She props her hands on her hips, all surly and aggressive, and my cock threatens to tear through my pants. Jesus. "Why not?"

"Because I'm not doing forty-to-life for murdering one of these perverts." I cup my hand around her neck and rest my forehead against hers. "Please cover up your tits. It's a holiday. Let's not muddy it up with quadruple homicide."

She sighs but ultimately takes the dress from me, pulling it grumpily over her head. "You're ridiculous. You're the one who picked this bikini out!" The cover-up is still see-through, mostly some kind of crocheted woven thing, but it's better than the alternative. She juts her chin out, challenging. "Better?" she asks.

"Much." I take her hand, linking our fingers together. "Now, what is it that you so desperately need from the marina shop that you just *had* to get for yourself? Because the chef can whip up anything you want in the galley, but I mean, if you're looking for shitty beer, this may be the spot to get it."

I know my girl. Something's been bothering her since we got on the yacht this morning. Killian and Rath are used to this side of me and my family—the expensive toys and over the top displays. But ever since all the shit that went down at the Mercer Family Christmas Ball, she's been uncomfortable around my parents.

She shakes her head, the annoyance falling away. That just confirms my suspicion. She's usually a lot more spirited in fighting back. "I just needed some air. And to put my feet on solid ground. That's all."

Nice try, sweetheart.

"Did someone say something to you?" I ask, just before we go inside. "Did my mother—"

"No. Your mother was fine." The way she says 'fine' doesn't inspire confidence.

I narrow my eyes, watching her carefully. "What about my dad? Because he's a prick in general, but shit gets worse when his fuckwit friends are around."

"No." She glances over at me. "Your family has been nothing but hospitable. I mean it, I promise."

The doors of the store open, but when she moves to glide through them, I grab her arm, dragging her off to the side. Leaning her against the ice machine, I touch her chin with my fingers, making her meet my gaze. "Tell me what's really going on."

She holds her stance for a moment, but it crumbles under the weight of my stare. "It's just... the fourth brings back a lot of memories for me."

"Oh." I run my hand down her arm. "Bad ones?"

Her mouth twists. "Good and bad."

"Okay," I say, not sure where to go with that.

Story exhales, looking away. "My mom loved the Fourth, and every year we'd come out here to see the fireworks. It was always a big deal for us, and even though we didn't have much money, she'd always try to make it special." A wistful expression crosses her face, her gaze falling. "We'd come early. It was the only way to get a parking spot–plus a good spectating spot with enough room to spread out the blanket on the public beach. She'd unpack a picnic with my favorites. Deviled eggs and fried chicken—"

"Posey makes killer fried chicken," I say, trying to tell her that it's okay.

It's okay to remember good things about bad people.

She smiles, eyes flicking up. "Yeah, she does." She twists her fingers into the woven dress. "If I was lucky, she'd have enough money to splurge on a glow-in-the-dark necklace and a rainbow pop from the vendor."

Fuck.

"She did what she could," I say, knowing that everything

Posey did was for her daughter—even if it was psychotic and misguided and basically more harmful than anything. She never wavered on this, up until the point she went to prison.

Story nods, shoulders drooping sadly. "One year, though, she got called in for... a job." *A trick*, I decipher. "She just couldn't say no–we needed the money too badly. But she promised it'd be quick, and even if we couldn't have the picnic, we'd still see the fireworks." I put my hand out to cover hers where it's wringing the fabric of her dress, bracing myself for whatever comes next. "I spent the night in the hotel bathroom listening to my mom—" She swallows the rest of the thought.

My stomach drops. "Fuck."

Story tightens her mouth in that way I've come to realize is an attempt to stave off tears. "I was so angry. At her. At the fucking asshole keeping her occupied. I didn't get it, though. You know? The reality of what was really going on? I just knew I was missing out on this amazing, fun night. Missing out on deviled eggs and a glow-in-the-dark necklace, and that one shred of stupid normalcy that we had one fucking night of the year." A tear falls down her cheek and she swats it away. "By the time she was done, it was already dark. There was no fucking way we were making it."

I wrap my arms around her waist. "If I could go back in time, I'd show up at that John's house and break his goddamn fingers, one by one." More pensively, I add, "You know, give me a description. I'll find him and do it now."

She laughs, giving me the watery smile I was hoping for. "Thank you, but it isn't necessary. We were on the way home from the hotel and were driving past the elementary school when, in the distance, the first fireworks shot in the sky." She looks upward at the clear blue as if she could see them now, her smile turning a little sweeter. "Mom swung the car into the school lot, popped the trunk, and got out a blanket. The front lawn was filled with families, but there was plenty of room, and we spread out and watched."

"So you got your fireworks after all."

She nods, sniffling. "We did. It was spontaneous. A great view, less traffic and… just a nice night." Some of the darkness slides back into her eyes. "It's just weird, isn't it? How a memory can be both terrible and amazing at the same time."

It's selfish of me, but I wonder.

I wonder how many terrible-slash-amazing memories she has about me. About us. How many moments could have been perfect, if only they hadn't been spurred on by something tragic and painful?

I look down at her, processing the story, and come to one conclusion. "You miss her."

She shrugs. "I shouldn't, but sometimes, on days like this, I really do." Leaning into me, body lax, I get the feeling she's expecting me to react a certain way about this.

I curl my arms around her assuringly. "It's okay to miss her. She's your mom."

Her body jostles with a silent laugh. "Well, six months later, she started dating Daniel and... well, as crazy as that turned out, I never would have met Killian or you or Rath if she didn't."

"And you would have never become our Lady."

She nods. "I don't regret my life—the easy parts or hard ones. It's just sometimes the memories are overwhelming."

Understanding, I realize, "Sometimes, you just need a rainbow popsicle." I reach back and grab the door handle. "How about I buy you one?"

"I knew I let you come with me for a reason." She bumps her hip into mine, her smile blinding. "Sugar daddy."

She's ridiculous and sexy, and when she puts that pop between her lips, I think I may actually come on the spot, but if I can give her one thing–a good memory, a little stability, a fuck-ton of love–then maybe this will be one memory she won't want to forget.

"THE CAPTAIN IS going to drop anchor in a few minutes," Dad calls out on his way to the upper deck. A string of men and women follow him, all dressed in white linen and boat shoes. My mother, or whoever works for my mother, has spread a massive buffet and bar on the deck below this one, while leaving the top deck for viewing. Cushioned chairs are arranged across the space and as the sun falls below the horizon, everyone finds a spot.

"We'll have a perfect view of the fireworks," I note.

After we got back from the store, with Story's lips colored a shiny red from the popsicle, my father pulled away from the dock and cruised down the river until he found a secluded cove. Always eager for a new sport, Killian took my dad up on the offer to fish as the sun went down. Story spent most of the afternoon in the water—her first time on a wakeboard, which I towed on the speedboat attached to the yacht.

The twins showed Story all the tricks; how to get up, how to hold on with one hand, crossing the wake. I love seeing them together, Story's bright smile along with my sisters'. They have friends here too, and the group of them are piled onto cushions closest to the edge, eating ice cream sandwiches and thick chocolate chip cookies.

When I stepped into the bathroom to take my shower earlier, Story and Rath were entering one of the bedrooms downstairs, no doubt fucking on my mother's white and blue nautical bed linens. They must still be at it, and I'm about to go down and find them—*join them*—when she emerges on the staircase, two glasses of champagne in her fingertips, still wearing that white bikini, although she's pulled the woven cover-up on top. Her cheeks are flushed, not just from the sun—I made sure my girl had on all her SPF's.

"Is that for me?" I ask, feeling loose and happy. Rath and Killer both come to the upper deck as well, finding seats a few feet away. I'd positioned myself farthest back in a deck chair with a perfect view. There was a time when I would've insisted on being the one to set off the fireworks, inhaling the scent of sulfur and my fingers itching to light the fuse. I guess after you've set a building on fire, fireworks lose a little of their appeal. Mostly, though, I want to be the one at her side when they start. I want to be the one to give her what she wanted in that memory: a shred of perfect normalcy. A happy memory without something terrible attached to it.

She trusted me with something back there at the marina, and it's fragile. That much, I know.

I intend to protect it.

Story hands over the drink and bends, kissing my lips. This is one of those events where she gets to be *my* girl. My parents have vaguely, and very conditionally, accepted my lifestyle, but they're not into me flaunting it in front of their rich friends or even the twins. I get it, and honestly, I like having her for myself for a little bit. She's Killian's Queen and Rath's private safe harbor. But here, in public, she's the woman on my arm, the girl who won Forsyth's battle to bag the next eligible Mercer.

Plus, it's not like she didn't just get railed by Rath down

below.

I chuckle. *Down below.* I bet that's where Rath gave it to her. Jesus, he's obsessed with her asshole lately.

"What's so funny?" she asks, propping her hip against the chair. I run my hand up her leg, beneath the cover-up, and finger the elastic of her bikini bottoms.

"Nothing," I say, keeping my dirty thoughts to myself. I'm having less control with my hands, teasing the skin beneath the elastic. "Have a good day?"

She hums, adjusting her thighs to greet me. "Yeah. You know, Daniel had money, but he never spent it on anything fun." Her voice turns sour. "He was too busy trying to control and manipulate everyone."

"Sounds right." The sun slips behind the horizon, splashing the boat in reds and pinks. She's just standing there all perfect and sexy *and*—I push my fingers under her suit and brush her clit. Story's spine straightens but her legs part for me. I hide my smirk with a sip of the champagne. "Daniel never knew how to have a good time. Well, not unless it was at the expense of others. One reason my father never respected him." I circle the bundle of nerves, my cock getting hard when I feel the slick heat building. "The Mercer men, on the other hand, are all about having fun."

I've got my index finger poised at her entrance when I hear my mother's voice. "Tris, honey, sure you don't want to sit up

115

here with the rest of us? There's room."

"We're fine, mom." I smile over at my mother, her gold jewelry glinting in the fading sunlight. Both Rath and Killian have turned to face us. Killian's forehead creases, aware that something is up. Rath just gives me a nod of approval. I look up at Story, whose cheeks are even redder. "Right, sweetheart?"

"Y-" I push my finger into her pussy, curving the tip. "Y-yes, ma'am. We're good. Thank you for such a lovely day."

My mother frowns, eyes narrowing. Story's pussy clenches around my finger. "Story, dear, you're very red. I hope you didn't get too much sun."

"Mom," I call, "leave her alone. I'll get her some aloe."

I pump my finger in and out and feel Story's knees start to wobble. A strangled sound comes from her lips as she tries to maintain composure. She looks down at me and hisses, "I'm going to get you for this, you know that."

"Get me what?" I ask softly. "Horny? Congratulations," I run my hand down my shorts, feeling the bulge, "mission accomplished."

But I pull my fingers out of her pussy and grab her around the waist, dropping her on my lap. She lands hard on my dick, and I grunt, hands cinching around her waist. "For someone acting so put out, you're pretty fucking soaked."

"Tris," she says, her tone full of warning. But that's not all. I hear the whine under the words, the want.

I sweep her hair from her neck, whispering into her ear. "In a few minutes, my dad is going to tell the captain to dim the lights. The fireworks will start, and that's when I'm going to fuck you." I kiss the back of her neck. "You going to be ready for that?"

She turns her head, my nose skimming the cut of her cheekbone. "I'm ready now."

"I know you are, sweetheart. But you'll have to wait a few more minutes." I press my lips to her cheek, my cock throbbing. "Can you do that for me?"

She nods and I pull her against my chest. It gives me a good view of her tits, round and full under the fabric of her bikini top.

"Captain," my father calls to the man at the helm. "Dim the lights please."

Story laughs at the predictability, her body shaking against mine. I run my hands down her arms, grinning wickedly. "Two minutes until showtime."

When the lights dim, I set it into motion, cramming my hand down between us to untie my trunks. My cock is achingly hard when I pull it out, guiding it between her legs. Story exhales when she feels me against her, and I've just hooked a finger into her bottoms, pulling it aside, when a server approaches us with a tray.

"Champagne?" he asks, unaware that I'm half a centimeter away from pushing my way inside the woman he's speaking to.

Voice even and crisply composed, Story says, "Yes, please,"

and smoothly takes a glass. God, she's gotten good. The first time we did this, she panicked. Fuck, it was hot. But this is better. It's like having a partner in crime–a fucking wet-dream come true.

"Sir?" he asks, offering me the tray, I take a glass with my free hand and guide my cock into Story's pussy with the other. Her hips slide back, taking every slow, agonizing inch of me, and the waiter frowns. She just takes a sip, licks her lips and says, "Mmhmmm, so good."

The waiter nods and moves to the next couple, allowing me to refocus on the weight of Story in my lap, perched primly on my cock. I savor it more than the champagne I'm sipping, expanding inside of her wet, tight heat. The sound system, which had been playing bland, low-volume, ambiguously patriotic music for the last thirty minutes, cranks up right as the first firework explodes in the sky.

Story rocks her hips, but I still her, commanding, "This is how we're going to do this. No thrusting, no grinding, no actual fucking until this gets going." I glide my hand up her side and cup her tit. "You're going to just feel me inside of you until then."

"I can't," she says, words strained.

"You can and will."

Her pussy clenches, the instinct to fuck and thrust wired into us on a level that's so primal, it's almost impossible to hold back. But like a good girl, Story follows my directions, just letting me settle inside of her. God, it's painful—excruciating—but fucking hot.

I hardly notice Maynard Lockley, one of my dad's accounting friends, bounding down the deck until his footfalls grow close. Just my luck. This ancient fucker has a rep for droning on like a goddamn corpse.

I can feel Story stiffen as Mr. Lockley approaches, but I don't see it. She's good at pretending, keeping her gaze aloft as another explosion of sparks flowers in the sky.

"Tristian," Mr. Lockley says in his nasally voice. "Your father mentioned you might have some recording equipment stored down below. You see, my Marie couldn't make it tonight–her arthritis has been acting up with all the weather–so I thought I'd bring Scooter up here," that's her toy poodle, "and just get some video to take back to her, but my phone…" he pulls it out, tapping uselessly at the screen. "It's deader than a doornail, son. If I had some kind of–"

I stop him before we all die of old age. "There's a camcorder on the shelf beside the fridge." Stifling a smirk, I grab Story's hips, lifting her up. The sudden drag of my cock makes her breath hitch, hands clamping over my wrists. "Why don't I go and get it for you?"

As expected, Mr. Lockley shoots out a hand, head shaking. "Absolutely not. You sit here with your pretty young lady and enjoy the show! I'm sure I can find it myself."

Giving him a rueful smile, I lower her back down, my toes curling at the sensation. "If you're sure."

He flicks me a wave as he disappears down the stairs.

Scooter scurries to catch up to him.

"You're such a tease!" Story growls.

My cock jerks inside her, just as impatient as she is. "And you're my pretty young lady," I say. Along with the fireworks, the tempo of the music increases, and I rock up into her for the first time, tired of the game.

A gust of air bursts from her chest—like she'd been holding it in this entire time. "Oh," she breathes, rolling her hips against my thrust.

Pressing my lips against her ear, I whisper, "That feel good, sweetheart?"

She shivers. "Yes. *More*."

I look out over the upper deck, illuminated by another flash of sparks. "I know what you want, but we have to be careful. It'd take practically nothing for someone to realize what we're doing."

It's just as much a tease for me as it is for her. The thrill of possibly getting caught is half the fun. The idea that everyone here could look over at the same time, seeing that my dick is buried deep inside her, just makes me buck up into her again, her shoulders jerking in surprise.

"Watch the show," I demand, tugging her back into my chest.

"You'll get it when you get it. Don't I always take care of you?"

Obediently, she goes lax, thighs parting as she rolls her head against my shoulder, gaze fixed on the sky.

The fireworks are really something, but then they always are. It's just hard to care about them when I've got my girl in my lap, so beautiful and wet for me. Mostly, I'm just waiting for the booms that signal the big guns. They always start the fireworks out slow and easy, but the real show doesn't happen until ten minutes in.

By the time they do, Story is sweating, the slender column of her throat jumping with swallow after swallow. Her pussy flutters around me, clenching, like it's holding on tight, willing me to do something. I watch the flashes above reflecting in her heavy-lidded eyes, and when I look around me, I see the others are doing the same.

Absolutely everyone's rapt attention is drawn to the sky.

Showtime.

I grab her waist tight, lifting her the scantest inch, and then drive up into her hard and fast.

Her teeth clench on a whimper. "*Tris…*"

I answer with a grunt. "God, your pussy's dripping." I lick out to taste the salt of the sweat on her neck, but my eyes are fixed to the crowd, wide and alert as I plant my heels, fucking up into her. This is a new game–one of my favorites. How long can I fuck her like this, so brazen and obvious, before someone's head turns?

Seven thrusts, this time.

I drop her back into my lap as casually as possibly, watching a woman ahead of us turn to her husband. They share a laugh, but it's not long before they both tip their heads back to look at the next big boom.

Casting my eyes around, I catch Rath's gaze, the blaze of sparks in the sky glinting off his lip piercings when he smirks.

Obviously indulging me, he looks away.

I'm the one sweating when I lift her again, pistoning my hips up into her in a lightning-fast series of thrusts. The tendon in her throat tightens as she arches her back, jaw dropped.

"Oh my god," she raggedly whispers, working her hips tandem with mine. "Don't–don't stop. Not this time. Please, just–" Her voice cuts off when I slam her back down into my lap, laughing along with the group. It's a harsh, strained sound, but believable enough.

Mrs. Lockley's toy poodle, who apparently isn't a fan of big sky explosions, just dove his fluffy little ass right off the side of the boat.

She startles at the sound, her dazed eyes blinking at them.

"Scooter!" Mr. Lockley's shouting, trying to balance the camcorder. "Aw, hell, you stupid mutt! You just got groomed! Marie's going to have my hide."

"Dogs and fireworks don't really mix," I offer, raising my

voice.

Story's fingernails dig mean crescents into my forearms.

From across the deck, Killian coolly offers, "Hey, I've got a cage, if you need one." Mr. Lockley grumbles as he passes, flapping a hand.

For the span of time it takes for everyone to turn back for the next boom, Story's hips keep making these stuttering movements, like she wants to writhe and keeps forgetting she can't.

I wait patiently as their attention is recaptured, grabbing Story's waist and lifting her for another round of slamming thrusts. My calves burn with the rhythm, thighs flexing up into her as she bites down on a keening moan, rolling her hips against me.

She spreads her thighs wider, hooking her ankles around my legs, so entwined with me that every punch of my hips makes her tits bounce. My own eyes are on the spectators, assuring no one's watching as I dip my fingers beneath her cover-up, between her legs.

Her body is coiled tight, ready to spring, and when I touch her clit, she jerks forward violently.

"That's it, sweetheart. You can let go now." I whisper in her ear. "You've been such a good girl. I'm not going to stop this time. You understand?"

If someone looks, they look.

She drops her head back on my shoulder and nods. "Fuck me, Tris."

"My pleasure."

I plant my hands on her hips and lift her up before driving her back down. She grips the arms of the chair, giving herself leverage. The music blares from the speakers, the fireworks burst in a rainbow of color, and I bite down on her shoulder to keep from groaning.

Glancing up, I see Rath watching us again. He's always such a good audience for us. Never speaks. Never moves. There's just his dark, sinful eyes boring into us.

Rath is the best person to give a show to.

Indulging all three of us, I spread her thighs wider, glancing around to make sure everyone is still focused on the sky when I flip Story's dress up. His eyes instantly drop, taking in the sight of her sweet pussy as I fuck into it. An appreciative curve of his brow is all the reaction I get, but it's enough.

I press my thumb against her clit, rubbing. "Rath wants to see you come, sweetheart. You about ready?"

Her body shudders on top of mine, pussy slick as I drive into her. I lose sight of everything but the feel of her. The sounds of the explosions are nothing compared to the little cries coming from Story as I fuck deep into her.

She knows what I want, holding back until this final crescendo, and my girl gives it to me, picking up her pace as the display escalates, more and more fireworks bursting in the sky, explosions so bright I'm blinded.

When her shoulders lurch, thighs slamming shut with her rolling orgasm, I finally let go, coming more violently than I mean to. I shove her down–hard–as my teeth dig into her shoulder, stifling my growl.

My dick pulses wave after wave of hot cum into her, which is always the hardest part for me. There's no hiding the way it takes me, the clench of my jaw or the rapture I feel. Having done this enough times to know–I'm usually so much better at hiding–Story turns to kiss me, her slick tongue soothing away the blinding heat of bliss. To anyone else, it'd just look like a sweet makeout session.

I can still feel her pussy contracting around my cock.

"Mmm," I hum, breaking away to feel a passing breeze wash over my sweat-damp face. "You still taste like sweet cherries."

She gives a soft, breathless laugh. "Because of the ice pop?"

I give a lazy shake of my head. "No. Just you, sweetheart."

Just you.

WE
love
JUST AS HARD
as we
hate

ANGEL LAWSON
SAMANTHA RUE

LORDS

OUTTAKE

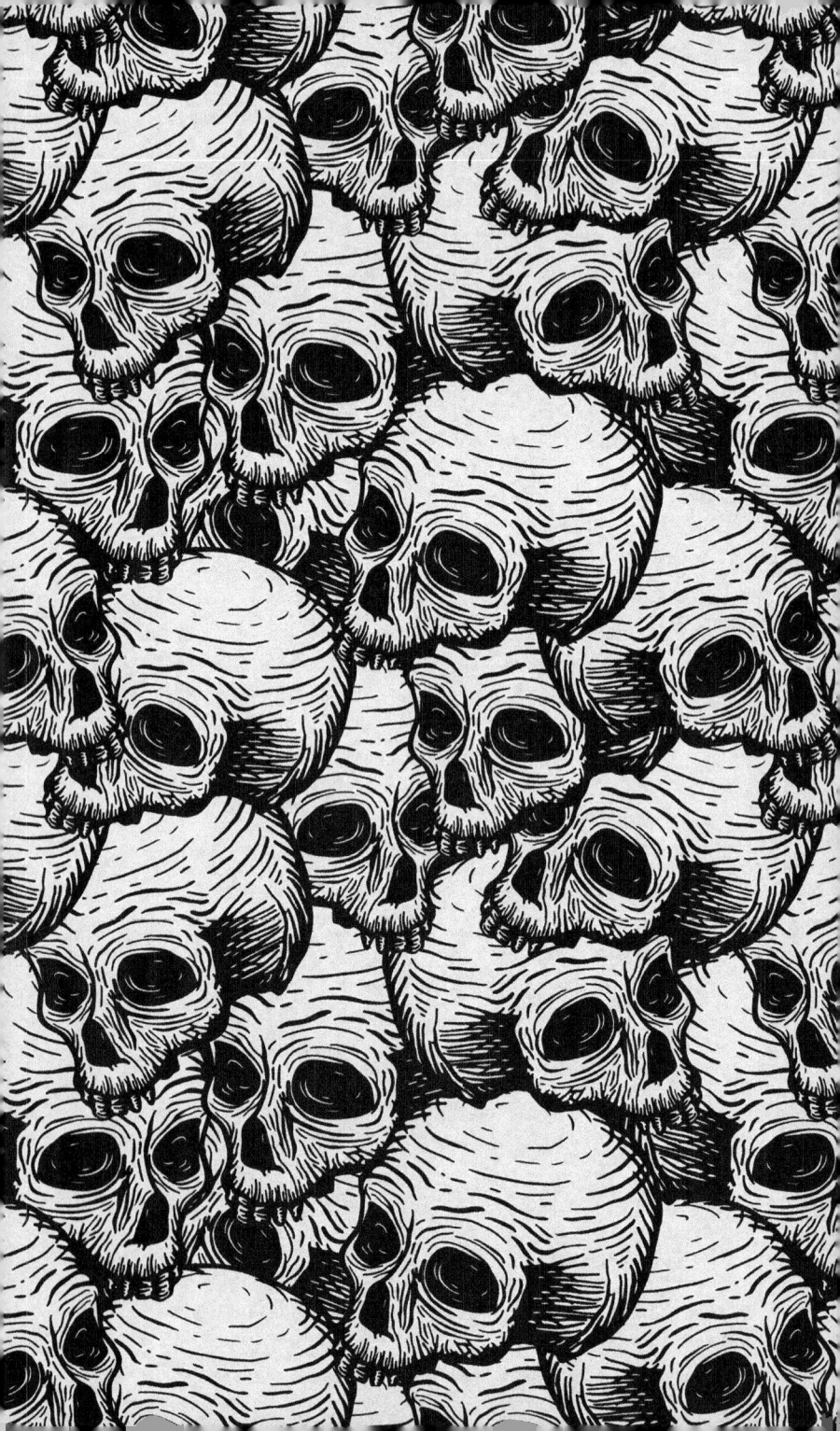

STORY

OUTTAKE

It's dark when I wake, startled from deep sleep by the nagging worry of something being wrong–out of place. I search my fuzzy brain, mixed up and confused from the weeks of interrupted sleep, when it hits me.

Shit!

The baby!

God.

I jolt up, heart pounding as my gaze darts to the bassinet that's been pushed next to the bed. She's not there. A second surge of panic runs through me, but I search the bed, finding Dimitri curled up on one side and Tristian on the other. *Killian.* I exhale a sigh of relief, realizing she's just with her daddy.

Squinting at the clock, I see it's nearly 2 AM, past time for a feeding, which explains the heavy ache in my breasts. She's never gone this long without eating before. I inch past Dimitri and Tris, working my way down to the end of the bed, making sure not to wake either of them.

Then I go in search of Killian and Melody.

It's been eight weeks since Melody was born. Even with their being four of us, we're all sleep deprived. The laundry is piled up in the hall, the sink is full of dishes, and South Side business hasn't slowed a bit. The guys continue to defend their territory, while working hard to create legal income. It's been slow and tedious, the tentacles of Forsyth linked in every aspect of business, but we agreed this is the right move now that we have a child to think about.

Despite how harried we've all been, a contentment has settled over the house. Having a baby clicked the last pieces of this complicated puzzle into place. I peek into the nursery, the dim fairy lights illuminating the room with a soft, warm glow. It's one of my favorite places in the house, decorated by Tristian himself. Three walls are painted a dusty navy gray, but one is sunny and yellow, bearing a mural of a cheerful meadow full of daisies, painted by the best artist in Forsyth–the same one who tattooed the daisy on my inner wrist–Remington Maddox. Even at night, the meadow seems to shine. Normally, I find myself searching the mural for the three skulls hidden within the flowers–one for each Lord–but tonight I'm looking for one Lord in particular.

The rocker and crib are both unoccupied.

I head downstairs, but it isn't until I reach the landing that

I see the blue light of the television flickering from the den. I descend, entering the dark room to see an old football game playing silently. Killian is sound asleep on the couch, head back on the cushion, clad only in a threadbare pair of jogging sweats. An empty bottle of milk sits on the side table and the baby is curled up on his chest, cradled among the tattoos and muscles. It's an adorable sight, one that both pulls at my heartstrings and creates a familiar spark of want in my lower belly.

In the last year, Killian hasn't exactly changed, but he's evolved. He's still a physical beast and just as mentally imposing as ever. He still has his fingers in a dozen pots, catching opportunities just as skillfully as he once caught footballs. It's been hardest for him to shift directions with the business, the Royal culture ingrained into his DNA. Once a Lord, always a Lord. The system seeps into everything in Forsyth: the university, the frats, the community. But my big brother is a good King. Powerful and determined. Benevolent when he wants to be, and ruthless when he has to be.

And with our baby?

He's merged into something else. An amazing dad.

Neither of us want to repeat the sins of our parents.

I step closer, watching Melody's sweet little body rise and fall on Killian's chest. Her lips suckle at her fist, and I start to reach for her, when I hear footsteps coming down the stairs.

"Hey," Dimitri says, eyes still puffy with sleep. His inky hair is messy and I know precisely how it got that way. We'd fallen asleep earlier in the middle of making out, pulling each other's hair, grinding slowly against thighs.

But it never goes farther.

It's been years since they've made the promise to never come anywhere but inside of me, but even through these last months–god, *months*–of me being unwilling or unable to have sex, they've kept it, seeming happy to let the anticipation build with early morning blowjobs and late night makeout sessions that might leave me frustrated if I had the energy.

"She down there?" he asks, and the closer he gets, the more I notice the undercurrent of tension in his features. Parenting with these three comes with its share of baggage. None of them are as neurotic as Tristian when it comes to Melody's wellbeing, but none of them are as paranoid as Dimitri.

I move to the side so he can see Melody and Killian.

My full breasts ache just being near her.

Dimitri pauses, the tension dropping from his shoulders. "Aw." The corner of his pierced lip quirks upward. "When he's like this, you can almost forget what a fucking psycho he is, eh?"

I drag my lip through my teeth, twisting to look at Killian. "Almost."

There's a beat of silence, and then Dimitri's low rumble, "Yeah?" He must have heard the thread of desire in my voice, because he slots himself up against my backside, his half-hard cock poking at the small of my back. He speaks into the soft skin beneath my ear. "You ready for some dick, baby?"

I got the all-clear from the doctor a few weeks ago, but I've been waiting. It's been years since my body hasn't felt like my own, and I don't like it. Tristan's the only one I've really talked to about it, but I think Dimitri and Killian can sense it.

Sighing, I touch his forearm, wound around my waist. "Maybe…"

He lets out a soft, quiet groan, reaching down to brush the apex of my thighs. "Then you're in luck. Big brother's got first dibs."

I twist, narrowing my eyes. "What was it this time?"

These three, competing for position, even after all these years.

"Game of pool. Killer wiped the floor with us." He doesn't sound to put out about it, moving around me. "I'll take her."

"You sure?" I whisper. "I was going to feed her, but it looks like he beat me to it."

"Of course he did." He kisses the corner of my mouth, tongue flicking out. "Tris and I can handle the next few hours. You two get some rest. Or, you know, get no rest at all." He smirks.

"Thank you." My heart swells as I watch Dimitri pick up Melody, curling her into his chest. They're a vision, her tiny body cradled against his lean muscle as he ducks down to press a kiss to her head. They're so good like this, taking turns with the baby, getting up with her and making sure I get as much rest as possible. They want to be involved—different from their own fathers—and it brings me a strange, settling peace. It makes me love them more.

When he's gone, I stand over Killian, trying to decide if I should wake him or cover him with a blanket and let him rest. He's had a long week forming a new, fragile alliance with Yolanda, who might not own any Forsyth territory, but still has a lot of pull here.

My eyes trail over his body, still packed with hard muscle. He's leaner now that he's not on the field, but more mature, more solid. Golden hair trails down his lower belly, vanishing under the elastic hem of his pajamas. He's undeniably sexy like this and that stirring I felt earlier intensifies. I bend and run a hand over his chest, feeling the warm heat of his skin.

Dimitri was right.

I'm ready.

The decision is made in a blink, and I reach below the oversized shirt I'm wearing–Tristian's, I think–and kick off my panties. Carefully, I push my hand through the front flap of his pajamas and pull out his length. He's thick in my hand, warm and soft, just like I remember. I stroke him several times, slowly coaxing his cock to life.

His stomach dips and he rouses, thighs flexing.

"Shhh," I bend to whisper, "go back to sleep."

I've heard those same words a million times, faint and dream-like, always just before I wake to find him buried inside of me. I never understood the draw of waking someone like this, not fully, not until now. I straddle his hips, slotting his cock against my entrance, and then I watch his face, brow furrowed as I slowly sink down. Instantly, I feel him expanding inside of me, growing as I take him in. A soft, sleepy rumble rises from his chest as I seat myself, but his eyes remain closed, face slack. There is something, though. A swell beneath my ass, his thighs stretching.

The fingers against my leg twitch.

Exhaling, I rock my hips.

I ride him slowly at first, unhurried and achingly deliberate. I spread my hands over his chest, tracing the tattoos and bending to kiss the puckered scar of the 'S' he'd carved there, years ago. It's faded with time, just like mine and Dimitri's, but if I brush my lips over it just right, I can feel every atom of the raised skin as if he'd made it only yesterday.

When I rise, his eyes flutter open to meet mine.

I'm gifted with a long moment of his dazed expression, eyelids rising and falling lazily as he looks down and registers what's happening.

He blinks faster. "Fuck." It's said in a rough, gravelly voice that's contrasted with the gentle graze of his fingertips over my hip. I rock against him and he wets his lips, eyes fixed to where our bodies meet. "Morning, mama."

The title gives me a thrill, sparking a hungry desire that urges me to increase my pace. His eyes flash hungrily, fingertips pressing bruises into my skin, and I moan so that he knows.

We can be like we used to be.

This body is still mine.

This body is still *his*.

Killian's hands move under my shirt, and then he surges forward, pushing it up and over my head. If I wanted to argue, I couldn't–not with the way he hovers in front of me, dark eyes boring into mine as he deftly removes my bra, freeing my heavy, swollen tits.

"Jesus, I've missed these." He stares down at them in awe, like a man finding water in a desert. "I can't believe you wouldn't let me play with them."

In the thick silence of the room, I tell him, "They're not sexy," feeling more like a cow than a woman lately. "And too sensitive."

"I can be gentle," he promises. He looks so sad, so desperate, curling his fingers to graze the side of my breast with his knuckles, that it makes me pause.

Well.

He did let me get two extra hours of sleep.

I roll my eyes. "Fine."

He immediately cups me in his hands.

The instant my nipples meet his palms, I hiss out a loud, "Yowww!"

He yanks his hands back, palms up. "Shit! Sorry," he says, eyes wide and worried.

"No, I'm sorry," I say, humiliated at the lack of control over my body. How unsexy I've become. "It's because I didn't feed her…"

"Look at me, Little Sister." Thumbing my chin, Killian pins me under his intense gray stare. "I thought I was dreaming before. You want to know why?" He pitches forward to pluck a slow, wet kiss from my mouth. "I've been dreaming about this for months. Watching you walk around here all day. Your legs." A palm, sliding up my thigh. "Your ass." His hand, grabbing, pulling me to rock against him. "The way your neck looks when you glance over your shoulder." His mouth, dragging a damp trail down my jaw. "You've never been sexier. *Never*."

More carefully this time, he cups my breasts, squeezing them gently. That's all it takes for the milk to flow—a sudden rush of relief as the pressure releases. I wait for the wave of horror and embarrassment, but it doesn't come. All I feel is reprieve, the receding ache in my nipples making room for the ache in my center. "That feels incredible," I confess, rocking my hips a little. He's still inside, hard and waiting, and he punches back, filling me up. Mortifyingly, I'm the one to let out a loud, desperate groan. "God, do it again."

His eyes flare with a heat I'm not expecting.

I'm definitely not expecting him to squeeze them together and dip his head, latching to my breast. It releases another gushing flood of milk and my jaw drops on a keen, fingers tangling in the back of his hair.

There's another deep, gritty rumble from his chest, only this time, I can feel it in the pit of my breasts as he consumes it, licking and sucking the droplets away. I shudder an exhale, unaware of how much I need it–needed *him*–to bring me relief. How insane to think that even after all this time, he could still find some new way to excite me. The heat between my legs turns slippery and hot.

"God, you're fucking soaked," he says, lifting his face and brushing his wet lips across mine. "Keep riding me like this, and you won't be the only one leaking."

The words set my skin on fire. I push down, taking him as deep as he can go, because *fuck*, I want it. Over the weekend, all three of them had taken turns fingering me to the edge of absolute madness, coming into their own palms and eagerly pushing it into me. But this is going to be the real thing, and I'm ravenous for it, the sensation of his cock pumping his release into me, claiming my body, filling it up.

I prepare myself for the pounding I see building in his eyes, but a shadow moves on the staircase, and I freeze, wondering if Dimitri's bringing the baby back down.

"What is it?" Killian asks, continuing to buck into me slowly. "You hear something?"

I shake my head. It's the stillness that tells me that it's not Dimitri and the baby, but someone else

Someone who likes to lurk in the shadows, watching.

There's only a slight flinch of movement, but it's enough for blond hair to catch the faint light. His blue eyes hold mine from his not-so-hidden spot on the landing of the stairs, and I sink my teeth into my lip. I have no doubt he's got one hand down his pajamas, playfully stroking himself, aroused from watching the two of us from across the room.

"Jesus," Killian breathes, jaw going slack. I realize he's feeling my arousal intensifying. It only takes a glance over his shoulder to have his belly bouncing with a chuckle. "Ah, I see how it is. You always get even hornier when he's watching."

"Rumor has it," I whisper, bending to lick against the seam of his mouth, "you beat him for the chance at first dibs."

He cups my breasts, happy to have access to them once again. "Pretty sure he let me win, though."

I roll my hips, drawing a grunt from his throat. "Why would he do that?"

"To watch this," Killian answers, voice matter-of-fact.

"Then we should give him a show," I demand, unable to take it anymore. "Fuck me." I run my fingers down his sharp cheekbones. "Make me yours."

Killian lets out a low growl, Grabbing my hips and lifting me off his cock. I whine in protest, but he just flips us, dropping me back onto the cushions as he takes himself in hand, guiding his hard cock through my folds.

Hovering over me, he punches forward, entering me with a powerful thrust. Instantly, his mouth returns to my breast, suckling and tugging at my nipple. Each release makes my pussy tighten around his cock as he plunges into me, my heels scrabbling for purchase against the muscular swell of his flexing ass. We fall into one another, just like all the late nights we've been missing, him powerfully consuming me, me willingly allowing it.

There's a moment, right before the tide of pleasure takes me, that I look into his eyes and see my past, present, and future. I see the stiff formality of the first night we met. I see that day in his truck when he first taught me how to shoot a gun, the rain dripping from his hair as he watched me, always hungry. I see the night he stood at my door and begged for forgiveness. I see him now, winding us all together, and I see him tomorrow, steadfast and resolute.

It's hard and painful and so good that it draws a cry of agony from the depths of my soul, because *this*.

This is home.

We're nose to nose when I come, and it's harder and more delicious than I remember it ever having been before. The hormones flush through me with my release, making me tremble with the force of it. From the staircase, I hear a low, rough grunt, and I know Tristian is staving off his own orgasm–waiting to give it to me, in whichever way I want it.

I dig my nails in Killlian's back, wanting him closer, my tits painfully pressed against his hard chest. Shamelessly, I beg. "Please?" I push a soft, coaxing kiss to the stubble covering his jaw. "Give it to me, Big Brother."

His forehead drops to mine as the orgasm sizes him. The sound he makes is more than feral, so animalistic that it makes some fundamental, instinctual part of me grow still until it passes. His shoulders jerk as he slams into the cradle of my thighs, and finally, I feel it–his cock pulsating as he fills me.

"I love you," he says, grinding out the words as he shudders. "Jesus *Christ*, I fucking love you, you know that?"

I answer truthfully. "Yes."

He rolls us over so he isn't crushing me, adding, "And I love her. This life. All of it. So goddamn much."

"I know," I kiss his neck. "I know this isn't easy for you–being a dad." His chest is still heaving as I curl against it, tracing the faded scar on his chest. "Yours sucked. Mine sucked. My mother–well, you know how I was raised. But together, with Tris and Dimitri, we'll do this right. I know we will."

We lay together, bodies pressed against one another. After Melody was born, the needs of the baby, the lack of sleep, life in general, led to me not wanting as much physical contact as before. But this feels so good, so right, being curled up against Killian's solid body, feeling his chest rise and fall as he works to catch his breath.

His fingers trail down the valley between my breasts. "You'll come to me the next time you need a release, okay?"

"I will," I say, not sure if he's talking about the milk or going so long between orgasms. "Thank you for that."

"Thank you for waking me up like a horny dream goddess." He pushes my hair off my neck, mouth curving into a grin. "There's no need for you to suffer over anything, Story. We're here to take our share, even if that means I've got to suck your tits until you come."

I roll my eyes. "Always sacrificing, aren't you Lord Payne?"

"*King* Payne," he corrects, but can't hold his stern expression for more than a blink. "But for you? For this family? I'd take a bullet." There's no wavering in his words, and there's no reason for him to say it–it's just how he operates. Strong, tough, and unrelenting.

I run my finger over his other scar–the one on his side. This one never faded and probably never will. It's proof that they'll always be Lords and I'll always be their Lady. Because we love just as hard as we hate, and if we made it over the thin chasm that separates the two, then surely we can make it through anything.

"You already have."

Printed in Dunstable, United Kingdom

67912542R00087